MW01687943

Wish Upon A Christmas Star

Wish Upon A Christmas Star

The McCarthy Sisters Series

Elle Douglas

TULE
PUBLISHING

Wish Upon A Christmas Star
Tule Publishing First Printing, October 2024

Copyright© 2024 Elle Douglas

The Tule Publishing, Inc.

ALL RIGHTS RESERVED

First Publication by Tule Publishing 2024

Cover design by Lee Hyatt Designs

No part of this book may be used or reproduced in any manner whatsoever without written permission except in the case of brief quotations embodied in critical articles and reviews.

This is a work of fiction. Names, characters, places, and incidents are products of the author's imagination or are used fictitiously. Any resemblance to actual events, locales, organizations, or persons, living or dead, is entirely coincidental.

ISBN: 978-1-964703-82-4

Dedication

To my mother and father, Monique and David Douglas, who have given our family a lifetime of truly magical and joyous Christmases.

Chapter One

December 22, 1978

THE MOMENT THE office clocks chimed five o'clock, the junior associates at Morgan and Reid LLP flicked off their desk lamps, packed their work bags, pulled on their winter parkas, and assembled in the law firm's front lobby, Christmas bonuses tucked away safely in their pockets. It was the earliest the group were leaving work since being hired at the firm. All the bosses had already made early exits to get a head start on their holiday plans, so the first years didn't have to worry about making an impression by sticking around any later than the official end of the workday, as they usually did.

The group of five recent law school grads would all soon disperse for a well-earned week-long break from their firm in downtown Calgary. Jasper and Nadège both had families in the city, so didn't have far to travel. Neal was hopping on a bus to Vancouver in the morning, while Anton was flying across the country to Fredericton where his family lived. Jeannie Carmichael was getting up at the crack of dawn to drive to Butterfly Lake in the Rocky Mountains for her favourite few days of the entire year.

But in the meantime, the first stop for the group was the Trumpet and Tartan pub, just around the corner from the Morgan and Reid offices, and the can't-miss Friday tradition for the group of young professionals. They'd never been able to make it in time to take advantage of the happy hour specials until today.

Jeannie ducked into the women's washroom on her way to join the group to apply the lipstick she'd bought at lunch that day. She'd heard from her boss's secretary—her best work friend, Margot Clemson—that Ben Kane, junior partner at the firm and Jeannie's longtime work crush, was planning to join them at the pub. Jeannie had popped out on her break to grab the lipstick from Woodward's department store at the corner, a nice pinky-red colour called Cupid's Cranberry.

She smoothed on a light coat of lipstick, finger-combed her hair, and noted how tired she looked in the mirror. It wasn't just the fluorescent lights. The days had been long and tiring ever since she'd started her job just over seven months ago. Expectations were high for the associates, and there was an unspoken understanding that there wasn't space for all of them to stay on long-term, so Jeannie's hours felt endless and unsustainable. She also knew she needed to put in that much extra to get noticed over her male counterparts, who had more in common with the bosses and conversed with greater ease in between meetings and at the coffee station.

But it was worth it. It wasn't necessarily the most thrilling work; in fact, sometimes it was downright dull, but she liked the impressed expressions on people's faces when she told them she was a lawyer, and the compensation was pretty nice too, as far as entry-level jobs went. If she were lucky enough to stay on at the firm, it wouldn't take long for the amount on her paycheque to grow, which she found thrilling. She admired the lifestyles the partners lived—the beautiful homes, nice vacations, and overall comfortable existence they could give their families.

Plus, she loved her colleagues, so these Friday socials had gotten her through the long and busy weeks preparing briefs, filing memos, conducting research, and doing her best to be seen and not heard during meetings where the partners were present.

She was the last to join the group in the lobby. Her heartbeat kickstarted in her chest when she saw Ben Kane leaning against the doorframe, talking football with Jasper, his light-brown waves peeking out from under his herringbone wool newsboy cap. He glanced up when she approached, his light-green eyes flitting over her outfit, then flashed her a quick and charming grin.

She returned the smile and took a deep breath before joining Margot and Nadège, who were flipping through the magazines on the reception coffee table.

Margot looked up as Jeannie approached. "All set?" She tossed the magazine on the table and pulled a red wool toque over her unruly brown curls, then stood up and leaned in to whisper in Jeannie's ear. "You look great! Tonight's your night. I overheard Alistair asking Ben if he was dating anyone and he said 'nothing serious.'"

"Shh," said Jeannie, looking sideways to make sure Ben hadn't heard them.

An innocent flirtation had developed between Jeannie and Ben over the past few weeks, and Jeannie was almost certain Ben was joining the first years so that he'd have a chance to ask her out. It would be the best kick-off to the Christmas holidays. They'd probably wait to have a date until the New Year. Or was the New Year's Eve gala at the storied Grey Spruce Golf and Country Club, where she knew Ben's parents were members, too much to hope for? The party was the city's most exclusive event and always made the society section of the paper.

Jeannie planned to be back from the mountains and at her apartment the day after Christmas—her roommate, Laura, was also going out of town, so someone had to take care of their grey tabby cat, Jazzy—so Jeannie would be in the city, available for a magical night out with Ben, with enough time to spare to shop for a gown for the event. She glanced over at him again to find him laughing at something Jasper had just said.

He was perfect for Jeannie. Tall, handsome, athletic, well-educated, and well dressed, she knew from Margot that his family was connected to big oil north of Edmonton. He'd gone to school in the United States at Dartmouth and was an accomplished ski racer.

Jeannie could just picture it. They'd live in the city for work, maybe in a riverfront home in the South East which would be convenient for getting to and from work but far enough away from the downtown to have some breathing room. They'd buy a ski chalet in the mountains, where they'd spend their winter weekends. Or maybe a place on the California coast, or in Arizona to escape the cold. Their children would go to a good public school and do horseback riding and art lessons on the weekends, and Jeannie and Ben would grow old together while earning the envy of all her friends for their fairy-tale life along the way.

Now he just had to ask her out.

Outside in the blustery winter evening, the small group hurried down the street toward the pub, which looked cosy and inviting from the outside and was already filled with guests.

Ben held the door for Jeannie, Margot, and Nadège, and Jeannie detected a glint in Ben's eye as she moved past him from the frosty outside air to the warmth of the pub, where a live band was in full swing. Their group was lucky to find the last unoccupied table.

The pub, which was really nothing special as far as pubs went, was decorated for the holidays: white poinsettia plants with a dusting of gold sparkles lined the bar, fresh boughs of evergreen draped the walls, and coloured lights were strung around the room, giving the whole space a cheerful and festive feeling.

Jeannie would have one drink, maybe two, then head back to the apartment she shared with Laura and pack to leave in the morning to join her family. Even if Ben hadn't been joining them tonight, she still would have waited until the morning to drive out. The mountain roads could be treacherous at night during any time of year, but especially in winter when snow squalls were always a threat.

The group chatted easily over their drinks, discussing their plans for the break and gossiping about some of the firm's employees. When the band played a song they all knew, they joined in with the rest of the crowd. The set was all well-known covers and set up karaoke style, where guests could sign up on a list at the front to join the band on stage to perform. More than once, Jeannie tried to make eye contact with Ben, and when she was successful, the playful grin dancing on his lips told her he was on the same wavelength as she was. She just had to get him alone.

So, when he stood up to go to the bar, Jeannie saw her chance. "One more round on me," Ben said to the group, "and then I've got to hit the road. I want to be on the slopes at Fernie by lunch tomorrow."

Fernie at Christmas. Very nice. Did his family have a place there, or were they staying at some kind of fancy resort where they'd retire after a day on the slopes in front of a grand stone fireplace to sip on White Russians? It sounded dreamy.

Jeannie straightened her shoulders, her window of opportunity narrowing. She had to talk to him before he left.

"Gin fizz for me," Jeannie said. "I'll help you carry the drinks."

She trailed Ben to the bar, where a pretty bartender with strawberry-blonde hair and big green eyes took their order.

"So, what are you getting up to for Christmas?" Ben asked Jeannie, looking over at her for a second, but mostly observing the bartender as she prepared their drinks.

"I'm heading to the mountains," Jeannie said. "My grandparents own a lodge in Keystone Ridge, so that's where I've spent Christmas every year of my life. The Butterfly Lake Lodge."

"Butterfly Lake Lodge, eh?" said Ben, his eyes still glued to the bartender. "Sounds cute."

"Here's the lager," the bartender interrupted, ignoring Jeannie and practically bending over double to pass Ben the drink, her low-cut top showing off a generous amount of cleavage. Jeannie glanced down at her own crisp white button-up, which was on the dowdier side of what she usually would wear out, but as a young woman at a law firm she had to maintain the utmost professionalism, and that started with her attire.

"Thanks," Ben said, grinning at the bartender and then examining the pint. "A perfect pour." The woman smiled back at him and started to measure gin in a shot glass.

"How about you? You said you're going to Fernie?" Jeannie asked.

"Uh, yeah," he said distractedly. The bartender slid the other drinks and bill across the bar to Ben, a coy expression on her face.

"Here, why don't you carry these," he said to Jeannie, not breaking eye contact with the bartender. "I'll meet you back there."

Cheeks burning with embarrassment, Jeannie carried three of the drinks back to the table and slid into her spot without saying a word. She tried to focus on the story Neal was telling the group, but her attention kept drifting to the bar. She saw Ben scribble something on the receipt and the bartender pick it up and tuck it into the tight pocket of her top, both of them grinning like fools at each other.

Unbelievable. She'd been passed over for a bartender.

Ben returned to the table, a satisfied expression on his face. Clearly he'd come out with the intent of getting someone's number, except it wasn't Jeannie's. Why had she even thought for a second Ben would be interested in dating her? Was it true that guys like him were threatened by successful women? Had she completely misread their interactions at the office? Or was he just plain not into her?

"Merry Christmas, everyone!" Ben said, clinking his glass against Neal's and Jasper's.

"Thanks for the drinks," Neal said, holding up his pint. "Cheers, everyone!"

Jeannie tilted her glass back and tried to drink down the lump in her throat, finishing half of her drink in three long sips.

She felt Margot's hand on her elbow. "Come on," Margot whispered, tugging at her. "Let's get out on the dance floor. He doesn't know what he's missing. Forget about him." The small, tiled area in front of the stage had filled up since they'd arrived, and the band had just launched into "The Chain" by Fleetwood Mac.

"You go ahead," Jeannie said, slumping back in her seat. She tipped her glass back again, emptying it, and looked at her watch. If she went home now, Laura would still be awake with her boyfriend, Stephen, and Jeannie would be forced to talk to them and watch them be all cutesy all over each other. No thank you. She'd have one more drink at the pub, take her time walking home, and hopefully by the time she got in they'd have gone to bed for the night.

With her purse slung over her shoulder, she went to the bar, but this time the one at the back of the room so that she could avoid Ben's future wife. The crowd on the dance floor had joined in with the band, belting out the chorus and pumping their fists in the air.

"I'll take a gin fizz," Jeannie said to the guy behind the bar, an older man with a scraggly beard and a leather vest who looked like he'd wandered in after a shift at one of the ranches outside town. Why couldn't Ben have ordered drinks at *this* bar?

She paid her bill as the band announced they were taking a break before the next set, then slid onto a stool and searched the crowd for Margot but couldn't see her. She turned back to her drink.

"Wouldn't have pegged you for a Foreigner fan," Jeannie heard from over her shoulder and turned to find the band's guitar player standing there with tousled chestnut hair and smiling eyes. He was holding a paper cup and had shed the jean jacket he'd been wearing over his white t-shirt. He was also panting a bit and had a huge smile on his lightly perspiring face. Clearly he'd been having fun up there.

"What's that supposed to mean?" Jeannie asked, although she wasn't terribly interested in the answer.

"It means I saw you singing every word to "Cold as Ice" earlier."

Jeannie put her drink down on the bar and turned to face him. "So what? It's a good song. And what does a Foreigner fan look like?" she asked.

"Not nearly as pretty as you," the guitar player replied without missing a beat. The cheesy comment would have normally bothered her, but she found herself more bothered by the fact that she liked how he'd said it. "Everett," he said, extending his hand.

She rolled her eyes anyway, then shook his hand. He had a firm, hot grip, with calluses on his palm from his instrument. "Jeannie," she said. She gave a tight smile, then turned back to her drink.

"When are you coming up on stage?"

"Ha!" she said. "That sounds like my worst nightmare. Not a performer."

The sides of his mouth turned up in a way that was decidedly cute. Okay, so the guitar player was hot. Or maybe she'd had one too many gin fizzes. "Any requests, then? For the next set?" he asked, sliding onto the barstool next to her. "Labatt Fifty," he said to the bartender. "Please, and thanks."

"I'm heading home, actually," Jeannie said. "As soon as I finish this drink." She took a sip and waited to be left alone.

The bartender passed Everett his beer, and he held it up to Jeannie in cheers. She paused for a moment, then reluctantly clinked her glass against his bottle. He had deep-brown eyes, and his mussed-up hair had a bit of a wave that fell just below his strong jawline. He was objectively handsome, but the whole bar-musician thing lost him way too many points.

"Shame," Everett said. He moved his stool a little closer, then fixed her with his deep-brown gaze, something Jeannie figured he did every night with whatever woman was sitting in whatever pub he was playing. "Hey, I've seen you in here before. You live close by?"

"I work around the corner." She also lived a five-minute walk away, but she wasn't about to share that level of personal information with a total stranger.

He surveyed her outfit. "School teacher? Banker?"

"Lawyer," Jeannie said, then shifted a bit in her seat to

turn away from him a little more. Could this guy not tell she just wanted to wallow in her disappointment in peace?

"Lawyer?" he asked. "I'm impressed. And you won't get up on stage? Isn't part of being a lawyer getting up and performing?"

"I'm not that kind of lawyer."

"Well, what kind of lawyer are you? I could use a little representation myself."

Aha. Jeannie raised an eyebrow, then turned back to face Everett. "Oh, so you're *that* kind of musician."

"Now who's making snap judgements?" he said, his eyes sparkling with delight. He was playing with her, and instantly her guards went up. She'd had enough of that type of the law firm's clients: rich and accomplished businessmen who thought they owned the world, flirting with her like she was some kind of doe-eyed airhead instead of the second highest in her graduating class.

She straightened her shoulders, all business. "Well, what do you need a lawyer for?"

"My will," he said. "Just turned thirty last week and figure it's about time to make sure my assets are well allocated. If I kick the bucket."

Jeannie had to a suppress a grin. *Assets?* The guy looked like the most precious item he owned was leaning up against the speaker on stage. "I don't work in estates. I do commercial real estate. But here." She pulled her business card holder out from her bag and passed him a card. It was Christmas, after all. She would be charitable. "You can call the firm's main line, and the secretary will connect you with someone." If he even had enough money to pay the bill.

He accepted the card and turned it over, examining it, then glanced up at her with those kind but slightly mischievous eyes and slid it into the back pocket of his jeans. He opened his mouth to say something, then one of his bandmates signalled to him from the stage. "Thank you," he said. Everett stood up and walked six feet to a bulletin board beside the bar and ripped off a little tab of paper from the bottom of a flyer, then came back to the bar and handed it to her. She glanced at the poster and saw that it was advertising his band. *Megapony.* How cute. "And here's my card," he said. "You ever want to get together and talk music, you give me a call. You've got good taste. Can I take you on a date?"

"Thanks," Jeannie said. *But no thanks*, she thought, and shoved the small rectangle of paper to the bottom of her purse. "Maybe." He was cute; there was no denying that. But she'd heard enough stories about musicians from her old roommate from her undergrad years at UBC who now worked in publicity at a record label.

Everett made for the stage, then turned back. "Oh, and Jeannie," he said, "the *Myosotis scorpioides.* It looks nice on you."

It took her a moment to realise that he was looking at the pendant hanging around her neck, a small charm with a pressed blue flower set in resin that her parents had given her for her last birthday.

"Forget-me-nots," he said. "They match your eyes."

Jeannie blinked. Okay, so he had a few fancy words in his vocabulary, and he wasn't shy about showing them off. Before she could respond, Everett had turned away again, so she watched as he made his way back to the stage, a slight nag tempting her to stay and watch the next set, but her watch read just after ten o'clock. Laura and Stephen would likely have retreated to Laura's room, and Jeannie had to get an early start in the morning. Her grandma would be waiting for her, all of the baking ingredients and equipment lined up on the counter of the lodge's kitchen. She couldn't be late.

Without saying goodbye to any of her friends, she slipped out the side door of the pub as Everett and his band launched into their second set. Her spirits had boosted slightly, and as she walked through the bustling street toward her apartment, she soaked in the festive atmosphere, the bright lights, ornate store window displays, and flushed cheeks on happy faces.

Ben Kane could sit on a yule log. Christmas break had begun!

Chapter Two

THERE WAS NOWHERE more magical than Keystone Ridge at Christmastime. The small mountain town one hour east of Calgary, population fourteen hundred, was nestled into the heart of the Rocky Mountains and could have been plucked right from a snow globe or sold as individual pieces in a Christmas village display.

The town's storefronts were all festooned with thick wreaths, compliments of the local business improvement association, and every fifteen feet along the sidewalk there was a tree made up in a different theme, each sponsored by one of the area's community associations. There was an outer space–themed tree, dripping in miniature planet ornaments and astronauts, with a rocket topper in place of a star; a baking tree with cookie-cutter ornaments, miniature whisks, and measuring spoons; and a superhero action-figure tree that would likely be a few figures short after unminded children passed by, their parents too busy checking items off shopping lists to notice their little ones had pocketed an early Christmas toy.

Contributors to the annual ice sculpture exhibition had

just finished chipping away at the final touches on their glittering and intricate ice sculptures under the pavilion behind city hall, and at the park at the end of the street, families were gliding down the big hill overlooking Butterfly Lake on their toboggans and brand-new GT Snow Racers.

As Jeannie drove through town toward the lodge, she made a mental list of the different places she wanted to drop by before everything closed for Christmas. Queen of Buns, for their sticky toffee buns (and to try for the hundredth time to get the owner, Heli, to share her recipe) and A Novel Idea to buy some paperbacks to get lost in over the next couple of days. The lodge had a sizeable library, but there were a few new-release mysteries that she planned to devour and leave behind to add to the collection. Finally, she wanted to go to CFNB 680, the local radio station, to surprise her friend Hector.

The Butterfly Lake Lodge was just a short two-minute drive from town, on the shore of the eponymous lake. In the summer, the teal-blue waters drew visitors from all over the world to marvel at the preternatural colour. In the winter, the lake froze over like a pane of glass you could stand on, and you could see all the way to the lake's bottom in the few days before the ice was coated with a sparkling layer of snow. In any season, it was the definition of majestic.

A wide grin spread across Jeannie's face as she pulled into the lodge's driveway. Strings of bright, colourful lights were hung across every last surface area and tree of the property, and a fresh dusting of snow made everything pristine and sparkly in the morning sunshine. She pulled her Ford Pinto into the parking spot beside her grandpa's old pickup truck.

She'd been counting down to this moment for weeks, as she did every year as soon as the Christmas commercials started to play on the radio. This year, however, her excitement was slightly tempered with a tinge of sadness that this would be the last time the Carmichael family would ever celebrate Christmas the same way they had since as long as she could remember.

After operating the Butterfly Lake Lodge since 1934—the same year the Sunshine Village ski area opened—Duke and Sue Carmichael were ready to retire. They'd spent forty-four years renting rooms to the seasonal ski instructors who over the years had started to flock to the area.

They hadn't yet sorted out their plans for what to do with the lodge, but they'd informed their young boarders—mostly from Australia, with a few from Eastern Canada, and one or two from the States—that this would be the last season their property would be available.

The town had also been put on notice that this would be the Carmichael family's final year hosting their traditional Christmas Eve party, originally designed to give their boarders, who were away from their families for Christmas, a sense of home and belonging on such an important day. Over the years, the party had morphed from a simple dinner and modest stockings for each boarder to a must-attend event in Keystone Ridge that was packed with community members eager to bask in the lodge's enchanting Christmas setting and indulge in Sue Carmichael's famous cooking and decadent treats.

Jeannie exited the car, the crisp winter air punctuated by the sound of clacking hockey sticks on the ice down by the lake, where there was a large rink shovelled out for the lodgers' use and anyone else's from town who wanted to challenge them in a game of shinny.

On Christmas Day, the rink would play host to the Keystone Ridge Christmas Classic hockey game. After five years of losing out on the title, Jeannie knew her grandpa was desperate to win back the cup from the Larson family as a way of capping off their final traditional Christmas at the lodge, and if Jeannie could buy the win for him as a gift, she would.

The sky was bright, the still-rising sun casting an iridescent sparkle across the snowbanks lining the driveway and snow blanketing the tree branches overhead.

Despite the Butterfly Lake Lodge's pristine beauty in its most basic, stripped-down state, Jeannie's grandfather's mission was always to have the most well-decorated property in the area, and folks drove from counties away to see his display every year. He capitalised on this attention by setting up a space for canned food donations at the base of the lodge's driveway, and he always collected boxes upon boxes for the local food bank.

Every tree surrounding the lodge glowed with colourful lights, and the railings of the porch were all covered with fresh evergreen boughs. Wreaths, thick with juniper and pinecones, hung in the windows from sparkly gold ribbons. A painted SANTA'S WORKSHOP sign stood near the walkway to the entrance, and the painted elves, Santa, and Mrs. Claus wooden cut-outs that Duke had made when Jeannie was five took their usual places where passersby could see them from the street. The lamp-posts were made up to look like candy canes with white-and-red ribbon wrap, and two wooden snowshoes were propped up against the sign for the Butterfly Lake Lodge.

Jeannie stood for a moment, taking in the beauty of the festive decor, and took a deep breath of clean, frosty air. The fireplace in the great room of the lodge was no doubt blazing, the sweet scent of burning pine and tamarack carrying through the crisp winter breeze.

She slung her duffel bag over her shoulder and balanced her laundry basket full of gifts for her family, only making it a few steps before the front door of the lodge swung open. Duke Carmichael appeared in the doorway. He wasn't much more than five feet tall, but what he lacked in height he made up for in his exuberant expressiveness and big energy.

"There's the Jean Jeannie!" Duke exclaimed. He'd been calling her the nickname for the last few years after the song had been such a hit on the radio. He was a huge music buff and the only person Jeannie knew from his generation who bought records ranging from David Bowie and Roxy Music to Sister Sledge and Heart.

"Hi, Grandpa," Jeannie said, passing him the laundry basket, which he put down on the porch right away and put out his arms for a big hug.

"Your grandmother's had everything set up since the crack of dawn. Come on in."

The lodge was warm and alive with the scent of cinnamon, butter, and unmistakable pine from the ten-foot balsam tree in the great room. A series of stockings dangled from the wide mantel: one for each of the Carmichaels, then ten more stockings for the boarders who would be spending their Christmas at the lodge away from their families. Thick flannel quilts were draped on every seat, and a life-sized carved Rudolph figure stood in the corner of the room.

Everything was as same as in Christmases past. *For the last time*, Jeannie reminded herself, a pang of sadness sharp in her chest.

Jeannie found her grandmother, Sue, in the lodge's kitchen. The light-filled space was full of industrial-grade appliances, but still maintained a homey feeling with shelves of knick-knacks on the wall, a grandfather clock in the corner, and a wall of windows that showcased the wide vista of the Three Sisters mountain range in the distance while she cooked for the boarders every day.

Sue was wearing her blue apron and grey hair tied back in a bun and was fiddling with the radio. When she looked up and saw Jeannie, her face broke into a wide smile. "You're here!" she said, crossing the kitchen and wrapping Jeannie up in a big floury hug.

"Hi, Grandma," Jeannie said. "Mmm. Smells incredible in here."

"I just got off the phone with your mom. Your parents are just down at St. Christopher's helping to finish filling the Christmas boxes." Jeannie's mom, a retired bank teller, and her dad, a former insurance salesman, lived at the edge of town in a small bungalow they'd purchased after Jeannie had moved out to go to university, so now when Jeannie visited Keystone Ridge she stayed in one of the lodge's rooms, which Duke and Sue kept reserved for her visits.

Sue tossed her an apron. "They'll be here by lunch. But in the meantime, we've got work to do."

For Jeannie, it wasn't work. She cherished this time spent with her grandmother in her kitchen, and this tradition was a big part of what she'd been looking forward to for weeks.

With Johnny Mathis's voice floating from the radio and the sun streaming through the windows, Jeannie caught her grandmother up on her life. They rolled out the dough for Sue's famous shortbread, which would be part of the annual competition at the Legion the next morning once the ice sculpture winner was announced. They melted chocolate for salted caramel and pretzel bark, then cut thin slices of orange peel for cranberry orange bread.

"And is there a special someone I should know about?"

Sue asked, looking up from the star and tree shapes she was carefully lifting from the rolled dough with a spatula. "Sorry, that's your mom's job to ask."

Jeannie flashed back to the night before at the pub and the stupid grin on Ben Kane's face as he flirted with the bartender. "No," she said. Her cheeks reddened with the memory of her foolishness. "Why, know anyone?"

"Well, as always, these boarders are as charming as they come," Sue said. "But most of them are too young for you now. And your grandfather would toss them out on the street if they ever so much as looked at you the wrong way."

Jeannie smiled to herself. The boarders were always good fun and, for the most part, polite and charming young men, most of them thrilled to be living abroad, spending a winter on the slopes before returning to Australia to start their professional careers. There was always one or two she'd had a crush on growing up, and in her teens she'd agonised over what to wear to the Christmas Eve party or how she was going to get their attention. Now she just enjoyed the energy they brought to her grandparents' lives, and she knew her grandparents were good de facto parents for the young men at a time they were so far away from home.

"I'm fine on my own, Grandma," she said.

Although it wasn't the whole truth. At twenty-eight years old, many of her friends had already married and had children while she'd been busy studying at law school and working hard to get noticed at her firm. Marcus, her only serious boyfriend whom she'd met in the summer between undergrad and law school, had declared himself sick of her devotion to her schoolwork and how often she turned down invites to join his family for a week in Florida in the winter or a camping trip with friends over Thanksgiving weekend in favour of acing an upcoming test. The small sacrifices were a no-brainer to Jeannie, but she knew if Marcus couldn't handle her working hard during law school, he certainly wouldn't be happy with the hours she planned on putting in during her first articling job, and then after that as an associate, so she'd broken it off.

Part of the reason Ben Kane was such an attractive option was because he fit into her work schedule just as nicely as he fit into her vision for the future. But clearly he had other plans for his future.

"Of course you are, sweetheart," her grandma said. She leaned over and gave Jeannie a peck on the cheek. "You'll make someone the luckiest man alive someday."

Jeannie fought the urge to roll her eyes. Time to change the subject, which no doubt her mother would bring up again within the first ten minutes of her arrival. "Is everything set for the party tomorrow night? Anything I can do to help?"

"I'll be making the ribbon finger sandwiches fresh in the morning, if you want to help me with that. The band's coming at seven, and guests at seven thirty. Same old, same old. I told your grandpa that it's a good thing this is the last year. We're getting too old to be hosting a wild party, but he started looking forward to this in August, so!" She threw her dough-covered hands up in the air, and Jeannie laughed. Sue loved the party just as much as Duke did and would likely be one of the last ones standing at the end of the night.

After Jeannie's parents arrived, the rest of the day was spent finishing up the baking and playing checkers and Parcheesi in the great room where the party would be held. Before an early dinner, which Jeannie's mom and dad had offered to make, Jeannie and her grandparents got bundled up to go for a walk into town where Jeannie was able to visit the shops on her list, then look at the entrants in the ice sculpture contest. Her favourite entry was a series of Canadian geese, sculpted to appear in mid-flight. The rest of the sculptures were equally impressive: a fairy-tale castle, a giant octopus with flailing tentacles, a polar bear wearing a toque, a centaur, and a steam engine lit from the inside with glowing blue floodlights.

Jeannie bought three paperbacks at the bookstore and dropped off a card and a box of chocolates at the radio station for Hector to give to his mother, who'd had knee surgery a week earlier and wouldn't be able to make it to the Christmas Eve party.

On the way back to the lodge, Jeannie hung back a few steps behind her grandparents, who were still sweetly arm in arm, although a little more stooped over and a little slower than she remembered.

It made sense this would be their last year running the lodge and their last big party. But it still didn't feel right.

Enjoy it, she reminded herself. There was no use wasting the holidays feeling sad about something that hadn't happened yet. She took a few quick steps to catch up to her grandparents and linked her arm around her grandma's free one, the boots of all three of them crunching along the snowy path back to the lodge.

BY THE TIME Jeannie woke up for breakfast the next morning, the boarders were already long gone for their shifts at the ski resort. They'd be back before the party began, flushed with fresh air, famished, and in full festive mode.

Sue had a piece of quiche Lorraine warming in the oven for Jeannie, and as soon as Jeannie sat down it was placed in front of her along with a mug of steaming hot coffee.

The kitchen phone rang. "That'll be your mom," Duke said. He stood up and crossed the room to the phone on the wall beside the counter. Jeannie took a long sip of her coffee, which somehow always tasted better in the mountains than it did in the city, and looked over to see her grandfather's confused expression.

"Well, that's no good. That's no good at all," Duke said. "You tell them we hope they feel better, and if there's any chance they could still come by, we'd welcome that." He hung up the phone. "Two of the three members of the jazz trio have food poisoning. They think it was the prawn cocktail at a wedding they played last night. And Marty's starting to feel a rumble in his stomach, so you know what that means."

"For goodness' sake," said Sue. She slid her glasses off and rubbed the area between her eyes. "Well, what can you do? We'll put some records on. It'll be fine."

But Jeannie knew this was disappointing news for her grandparents. While Duke had enough records to play through the party, there was something about having live music that added an extra-special layer to the atmosphere, and everyone always looked forward to it.

That scrap of paper the guitar player had handed her the night before. Where had she put it? Maybe she could call and see if the band were free.

But it was a dumb idea. They weren't going to drive all the way out of the city on Christmas Eve to play a little party at a lakeside lodge.

She pushed the idea out of her mind and set to helping Sue pack her shortbread for the competition. The pieces were so buttery that the parchment paper they were sitting on had gone completely translucent.

"WHERE'S GRANDPA?" JEANNIE asked. It was early in the

afternoon, a time when the lodge was quiet, the boarders still out teaching ski lessons to visitors from out of town.

"He's gone to lie down for a while," Sue said quietly. "He's slowing down a bit, honey."

Jeannie flinched. Of course, her grandfather was in his senior years. But the idea of him slowing down meant that there was a chance that not only was this going to be the last Christmas at the lodge, but that there would be a Christmas one day without him there. The idea summoned a lump in her throat.

She had imagined spending every Christmas for the rest of her life at the Butterfly Lake Lodge with her grandparents, her parents, extended family, the boarders and community members, and someday not too far in the future, a husband and children of her own. Okay, so it would be a different type of Christmas next year, but the idea that Christmases with her grandparents were limited shouldn't have caused the tug on her heart to be such a surprise; maybe she'd just avoided ever thinking about the inevitable.

The timer on the oven went off, and Jeannie opened the oven door just enough to see that the cranberry orange loaves had risen perfectly, with just the right amount of golden crust on the top. She pulled them out to set on a cooling rack, watching out of the corner of her eye as her grandmother scraped the last bit of dough from her silver mixing bowl and then dusted her rolling pin with some flour. She was still moving well. Spry. Maybe there was nothing to worry about just yet.

Regardless, Jeannie was resolved to do whatever she could to make this Christmas as perfect as she could so she would never have any regrets.

Starting with the party that night. It had to be amazing.

"I'll be back, Grandma," she said. "I just want to wrap a few gifts in my room."

She ascended to the second-floor bedroom that her grandparents kept free just for her. It had a double bed with an oak frame and a large blue-and-yellow quilt, a dresser to keep some items so she didn't need to pack every time she visited, and a vanity dresser that had her favourite framed photographs from over the years.

Her purse was hanging from a hook on the back of the door. She rummaged around in it and extracted the envelope her boss had given her the day before that held her bonus.

She double-checked the amount in the envelope: three crisp fifty-dollar bills. Her plan had been—fingers crossed—to spend the money on a New Year's Eve gown, but now she'd only be dressing to impress Jazzy the cat on the 31st. She tucked the money back into her purse, then rummaged a little deeper beneath her wallet and her pocket mirror and found the little slip of paper she was looking for right next to the Cupid's Cranberry lipstick.

Quietly, she descended to the lodge's office and shut the door behind her, then picked up the phone and started to dial, crossing her fingers for a Christmas miracle.

Chapter Three

"HEY, PASS ME a Big Red," Everett called toward the backseat, his eyes on the highway ahead. Last night's gig had been a late one, and the sugar would help him keep his focus on the rest of the drive out of the city. The car he was driving belonged to the other guitarist, Greg, who was nursing a hangover in the passenger seat.

Everett took a sip of the bubble gum–flavoured soda, cold from having been in the car overnight, then he flicked on the radio to get the forecast for the day, even though he knew the weather would be the same as it always was in this area in December. Cold. Snow. After the announcer from CKXG confirmed this, Everett slipped a tape into the deck and sat back for the remainder of the hour-or-so drive to Kananaskis Country in the Rocky Mountains of Alberta. He'd been to the area a million times with his dad and his Boy Scout group as a kid, but it had been several years since he'd been there. Situated a few hours away from the city, the change in scenery was definitely welcome after back-to-back shows in pubs and small concert venues for the last few weeks.

It hadn't been hard to convince the rest of the band to take the last-minute gig. Greg's family didn't celebrate Christmas, and Patty, the bass player, just plain loved money and would do anything to make a buck. Kenneth, the drummer, was the only one who'd needed some encouragement, but they promised to have him back at his girlfriend's place shortly after midnight.

Christmas with Everett's family was always up in the air anyway, depending on his mom's relationship status with whatever loser she was dating at the moment and how many kids that boyfriend had, as well as if Everett's sister, Jessie, were well enough to leave the house that day and face the world. If anything, Everett would bring a pizza over to Jessie's place later in the afternoon and not acknowledge the fact that it was Christmas, or else risk sending his sister into a guilt-ridden spiral over the fact that she hadn't managed to buy presents this year.

They'd had a few great Christmases as kids when his dad had still been around, but the memories from those years felt like watching home videos of someone else's family. After his dad had passed, things had never been the same, and Everett was content to let the rest of the world enjoy the event. For him, it was just another date on the calendar. This gig was going to be a great distraction.

Plus, there was the fact that the pretty girl from the bar was going to be there. He didn't quite get what the party was all about, but she'd assured him they'd pay the band's rate in cash, plus a travel bonus, and there would be all the food they could eat and as many drinks as they wanted. Sounded pretty good to him.

The band's gear was piled into a small trailer hitched up to Greg's AMC Gremlin, which barely fit all four guys. Greg was in the passenger seat next to Everett, and Everett was trying not to be annoyed that Greg was scratching lottery tickets and getting silver dust all over the seat, even though it was his car. Patty and Kenneth were in the back arguing over the set list.

Just like when he'd been a kid, the section of the drive when the mountain range was no longer in the distance but felt like it was rising up around them in real time from the earth stirred a deep sense of excitement in him. "Where'd you say the turnoff was?" Everett asked Greg.

Greg pulled the fold-out map from the glove compartment and ran his finger across to section B-7. "Four more exits. Then it's a straight shot. The road will take us right to the lake." He reached over and took Everett's pop can from the cup holder and took a long swig.

"Gross, man," said Everett.

Greg ignored him and took another sip. "Remind me how you booked this gig again?"

"Just a little targeted marketing," Everett said, thinking about the way Jeannie's eyebrow had raised just slightly when he'd passed her the tab of paper from the poster, like she knew exactly what he was up to but would play along.

She wasn't just pretty. He could tell right away after meeting her that she was whip-smart, and not just because of the title on her business card.

Maybe this time he'd get her real number.

Greg let out a loud belch, and Kenneth answered with another even louder one.

With the company he kept, maybe not.

THE BAND PULLED into the Butterfly Lake Lodge's parking lot shortly after five p.m., just after the sun had disappeared behind the peaks of the mountains across the lake. The place could be seen from a mile away, glowing with kitschy Christmas spirit. Everett wouldn't have been surprised if there were a tree farm or a reindeer compound or something in the back.

He put the car in park but left the engine running. "I'll go in and get the scoop," he said to the guys. "You wait here."

The air was several degrees colder than in the city, so Everett zipped up his parka as he ascended the wooden steps to the lodge's entrance and clacked on the door four times with the brass knocker. Moments later, a short man with wispy silver hair and a sturdy build swung open the door. He was wearing a dress shirt with a grey cardigan over the top and was holding on to a string of bulbs. Based on what Everett had seen outside the lodge and inside its foyer, he was concerned the old man was about to blow the power to the entire county if he plugged in one more set of lights.

"Hi, I'm—"

"You're early!" the man said, narrowing his eyes. "Party starts at seven thirty. Sue's still getting set up—she'll kill me if I start letting people in."

Before Everett could respond, Jeannie Carmichael descended the staircase in the foyer behind him in a pair of bell-bottom blue jeans and a blue knit sweater with tiny white snowflakes on it and flashed Everett a quick smile and wave before taking the old man by the arm. "Well, it was supposed to be a surprise, Grandpa," she said. "But look! I found you a band!"

So, this was *grandpa's* party? Judging by the man's age, Everett was concerned. Megapony didn't know any Sinatra, and while they could probably improvise an Elvis Presley song, he didn't know they'd be walking into a senior centre's dance.

"A band?" the man asked. "How did you—"

"You'll love them, Grandpa." Judging by the expression on Grandpa's face, Everett wasn't so sure that would be true. Jeannie, however, appeared delighted. She also looked stunning, her dark hair tied back from her face in a ponytail. "Hey, Everett," she said. "Thanks for coming up. This is my grandfather, Duke Carmichael."

"Hey, Jeannie," Everett said. "And nice to meet you, Mr.

Carmichael." He shook Duke's hand, then looked back at Jeannie, admiring the way small pieces of hair hung loose around her face, her cheeks pink like he'd caught her in the middle of something. Instinctually, he opened up his mouth to compliment her, then remembered her grandfather was right there. "Thanks for inviting us," he said instead. "The rest of the band's just out in the car."

His gaze travelled past her down the hallway to a long table with a festive table runner going along the length of it. The table was covered with crystal wine glasses, glistening champagne flutes, a big silver bucket filled with ice, and a large candelabra right in the middle of it holding tall candlesticks waiting to be lit. When Jeannie had called to give him a quick rundown on the event, Everett had thought she'd said something about the place being like a boarding house for young men. With its prime location on a lake with a snow-capped mountain backdrop, Everett's first peek into the elaborately decorated lodge felt like he'd just stumbled into a stately home right out of a Norman Rockwell painting. "You didn't tell me it was going to be such a fancy party. We're—" He looked down at his ripped blue jeans and the plaid button-up peeking out from the collar of his parka. "We're not really dressed the part." He cleared his throat. "And, uh, sir, your granddaughter did tell you what kind of, uh, band we are?"

"I have a very discerning taste, my boy. What is it that you play?"

Uh oh. Were they about to be sent packing on the highway back to the city? The only way Everett wanted to drive another hour on Highway 1 was with a few crisp bills lining each band member's pocket.

"What did I tell you, Grandpa? You'll love them!" Jeannie sounded genuinely enthusiastic, which Everett was happy to hear, but something told him it wasn't enough to convince Grandpa.

Duke looked Everett up and down, a stern look in his eyes. "My boy. Tell me you know something off the new Kinks album. And you can get right back in that car and drive home if you don't plan to get the Led out tonight." He turned to Jeannie. "Now, why have we been hiring that boring jazz band every year? *This* is going to be a party!"

Everett grinned and took a glance back at Jeannie, who was beaming at Duke with all the love in the world. She gave her grandfather a kiss on the cheek.

"Sir," Everett said, "I think we've got you covered. Now, where should we set up?"

Chapter Four

BACK IN THE kitchen, while the band loaded in, Jeannie surveyed the mountainous platters of food her grandmother had spent all day putting together with Jeannie's and her mother's assistance. There were cream cheese pinwheel sandwiches, large ramekins of baked mac and cheese, and individual hand-held French onion soups waiting to be broiled at the last minute before guests arrived.

Later in the evening, the dessert trays would be rolled out: the melt-in-your-mouth shortbreads that had tied for first place at the Legion earlier that day, chocolate peanut butter marshmallow squares, Hello Dollies, and miniature crème brûlée tarts.

Jeannie plucked a few grapes from a fruit and cheese platter, then went upstairs to get ready for the party.

There were two outfits to choose from for the evening, and whatever she didn't wear tonight she'd wear for Christmas dinner.

She plugged in her hot rollers, then pulled the dresses from her overnight bag. The first was a nice pinafore style dress in a red tartan. She held it up, inspecting it, then frowned. What had she been thinking? It was a dress for a nine-year-old posing for a family Christmas portrait at Sears.

The second was much more revealing than what she was used to wearing: a form-fitting dress with little red sequins sewn into it. Margot had convinced her to buy it when they'd gone shopping at the Stephen Avenue Mall after work one day. The neckline dipped lower than she was comfortable with, and the short hem was...*short.*

She glanced at her watch. Kayley's, the women's clothing store in town, would be closed by now, so unless there was a miracle hanging in Sue's closet, red sequins it was.

Jeannie pulled the dress over her head, then carefully rolled her hair in the hot rollers and applied some light make-up. Anything too dark, combined with her dress, would make it look like she was heading to the Pink Panther Club in downtown Calgary rather than a community gathering.

A knock sounded at her door. "Come in," she said.

Her mother popped her head through. "Wow, that's quite the get-up," Gloria said, her red lips curling down in disapproval. "Where's that lovely blue silk I sent you from Eaton's?"

"It's at the cleaner's," Jeannie lied. She wasn't about to tell her mother she'd dumped the blue silk in a Goodwill donation pile during her last spring cleaning.

Gloria was dressed in a long patterned caftan dress, her signature emerald earrings sparkling next to her dyed auburn hair, which was styled in a layered flip. She was the most glamorous woman in Keystone Ridge, a woman who belonged in the city but had chosen love and settled for a life in the country.

She crossed the room and began fussing with the collar of Jeannie's dress. "So, the Morrisons are coming tonight," Gloria started, and Jeannie groaned.

"Mom, I will *never, ever* date Lincoln. I know the Morrisons are your best friends, but I find him repulsive."

"He's grown up a lot," Gloria said, reaching to adjust the rollers in Jeannie's hair. Jeannie swatted her hand away. "And honey, you're turning twenty-nine next year!"

"Do I have to remind you his nickname was Stinky Linky?" Jeannie said pointedly. He'd earned the nickname both from a chronic case of halitosis and cemented it the year he'd peed his pants in the car on a day trip to Yoho National Park.

"That was almost twenty years ago. He's gotten to be quite handsome and popular around here. And he's going to inherit the resort," Gloria said. "You know what that means."

"I'm making my own money at my job," Jeannie said. And she planned to continue doing so, eventually as partner at the firm one day.

"You won't want to work forever once you have kids. Trust me. You be nice to him tonight. Your grandparents are just as worried about you as I am. It'll make them happy."

Of course her mother had to play that card.

"Fine, I'll be nice. But that doesn't mean I'm ever going out with him. I'm not kidding. I'd sooner be single for the rest of my life."

"Well, let's just hope he doesn't get the wrong idea from that dress then," Gloria said, returning to the doorway. "We might have already told him you were excited to see him. Ta!"

Jeannie grumbled under her breath as Gloria disappeared down the hallway. She should have just fabricated a love interest in the city so her mother would leave her alone.

How pathetic that she needed to make up a boyfriend.

She pulled the rollers from her hair, combed everything into place, then went to join the party.

At least the music would be good.

THE LODGE DIDN'T necessarily scream rock and roll, but it had been a long time since Everett had been in a place so festive on Christmas Eve. As he descended the porch steps to collect the last of the gear from the parking lot, he did his best to ignore the familiar pangs of nostalgia that always seemed to surface at this time of year.

He pulled a speaker from the trailer and lugged it inside to the side of the stage, then started to fiddle with the set-up of the equipment for the best acoustics.

An hour later, the tech was sorted, and they'd made a few tweaks to account for the ceiling height of the great room, which boasted twenty-foot ceilings and what Everett guessed was an amazing view of the lake when it wasn't dark. Instead, blazing firepits surrounded by blanket-covered chairs were visible from the windows, and the room itself was filled with a warm glow from the fireplace and the twinkling lights on the huge tinsel-covered balsam fir on the other side of the room.

When Sue invited the band to the kitchen for something to eat before the guests arrived, Everett hung back to tune his guitar. He still wasn't entirely sure how their set list would go over with the crowd, although Duke was clearly a music enthusiast.

"It gets wild in here," a voice sounded from the doorway.

Jeannie had changed out of her jeans and sweater into a knockout of a sparkly red dress. Her hair was now loose from her ponytail and fell over her shoulders in a way that made Everett's heart skip right up into his throat. She had a playful smile on her pink glossy lips. He'd never seen such a beautiful woman.

She approached where he was standing and perched on one of the speakers he'd just set up. Everett did his best not to fix his gaze on the hem of her dress, which showed off her legs quite nicely.

"Is that right?" he managed to say. What he wanted to ask was what her version of wild was.

"Last year we had to buy all new lampshades for this whole floor after they became popular party hats. My grandma won't let a single bottle of hard liquor through the door this year. Only beer and wine. The Aussies…they're a good time. And the rest of the town knows how to tie one on too."

"Sounds like my kind of people."

Jeannie raised an eyebrow. "I figured."

He put his guitar down and looked at her straight on. "Now who's making snap judgements again?"

Jeannie grinned. "Fair enough." She stood up. "Are you coming to get something to eat, or what?"

Everett's stomach growled. Whatever was cooking in the kitchen off the great room was smelling pretty spectacular, but he wasn't sure if he'd get Jeannie alone again for the rest of the night. Or ever, maybe. This was his chance.

He was about to speak when a large commotion sounded from the front entranceway, and Everett turned to see four men in ski suits, all wearing Santa hats and holding gear bags and cases of beer, laughing and shouting about some kind of ski jump one of them had pulled off.

"I'll take it those are the boarders?" Everett asked.

"You got it," Jeannie said, grinning. "Life of the party."

One of the guys bounded over from the entrance, while the other three retreated upstairs. "You made it!" the young twenty-something said. He had a blond ponytail and wore a bright-turquoise ski suit that matched his blue eyes.

"Hey, Archie!" Jeannie said. She turned to Everett. "This is Archie. It's his third year staying here. He's Grandma's favourite."

"After you, of course," said Archie. "Merry Christmas, Jeannie." He turned to Everett. "Nice to meet you, mate," Archie said, shaking Everett's hand. "I heard a rumour about a proper band from the city. This guy cracking onto ya?" he asked Jeannie.

Trying my best, Everett thought.

Jeannie smiled. "He's behaving himself."

"So far," said Everett. "But I've heard the boarders bring the fun."

Archie grinned. "You know it. Well, you call if you need me! I'm going to go chuck these in the esky," he said, nodding toward the case of beer in his hands. "Looking forward to the show!"

Archie left, and they were alone again in the great room, but the clatters from the kitchen and the sounds of people moving through the lodge filled the place with infectious energy. It was an odd collection of people under one roof, but Everett found himself excited to play for the party.

"I'm going to get something to eat," Jeannie said. "Need anything else?"

"I think I'm all set," said Everett. "But wait. You said you owed me big time for filling in so last minute." He leaned his guitar against the makeshift stage and took a seat on the other speaker.

Her eyebrow raised again in that adorable way he'd seen at the bar, and it was everything he could do to keep himself from reaching out and tucking that silky strand of hair behind her ear. "Did I? I don't remember that. I remember us negotiating a fair rate, and you exchanging in a mutually beneficial contractual agreement."

Everett laughed. "Is that right? Maybe next time I should get everything you said in writing." He watched as she moved toward the bookcase, plucked a book off the bookshelf and flipped through it, then put it back in its place. "What I'm hearing about lawyers is true."

Jeannie turned to face him. "And what's that? I'm sure nothing I've never heard before."

"Deceitful."

A look of mock horror came over her face. "Never."

"Well. I seem to recall making an offer. And I just want to remind you about my offer. I'd like to take you on a date." Although where he'd take someone like Jeannie Carmichael would take some consideration. She'd been okay to go to a neighbourhood pub, clearly, but a woman with hair that glossy? With a business card? He had no doubt she'd have certain expectations of a first date, which probably meant the kind of places he tended to avoid.

For a moment it seemed like Jeannie was going to reject him right to his face. Instead, she started walking toward the kitchen, then turned back at the last second. "Play my favourite dance-floor song, and you've got yourself a deal."

With that, she disappeared behind the door.

"Oh, come on, that's not fair!" he called, but she was gone.

Sitting alone in the great room, Everett couldn't help but laugh. He liked Jeannie. He liked her a lot. He also liked a challenge.

It might take a Christmas miracle to figure out the song, but he was game.

BETWEEN THE DINNER and the party, Everett asked Sue if he could use the phone.

"I've got one in the office where it'll be a bit quieter. Right in here, honey," Sue said, leading Everett to a small room off the lodge's foyer. There was a desk with files and papers all over it, a bit of a mess, but it appeared there was some kind of a system in place. The wall was covered with framed family photos, advertisements for local events from over the past few decades, and painted landscapes of the mountains and lakes of the area. Sue caught him looking at a picture of Jeannie standing on the dock in a yellow bathing suit, sunglasses, and a baseball cap, holding a bottle of Coca Cola and smiling widely.

"You've met our Jeannie, then," Sue said. "Our pride and joy."

"Yeah, she's great." Maybe Sue could help him out. He

cleared his throat. "Hey, any idea what her favourite song is?" he asked. "To dance to?" No harm trying.

Sue raised an eyebrow. "Not sure, no," she said. "Why do you ask?"

Everett paused. He probably shouldn't tell her, but there was something trustworthy about the woman. "She told me she'd only let me take her on a date if I guessed."

Sue let out a hoot. "That's my girl, all right. She's a firecracker. I'll leave you here. So, you're not calling a girlfriend, then?"

"Nah, no girlfriend for me," he said. "Just...family stuff. It's complicated."

"Every family has something," said Sue, her expression softening.

"I don't know. Yours seems normal. Pretty much the opposite of mine."

"Well," Sue said, "I'll leave you to it. Take as long as you need." She exited the office and closed the door behind her.

But this would likely be a short conversation.

Everett steeled himself and dialled his mother's phone number. A male voice answered on the third ring. "Yeah?"

"Is that Jason?" Everett asked through gritted teeth. The low rasp and slow drawl could only belong to one short-on-IQ loser. Jason was the on-again, off-again boyfriend, and Everett was just waiting for his mother to realise she'd be much better off turfing the guy to permanent off-again designation.

"I'll get your mom," he said, and Everett winced as the phone clattered onto the counter.

He could hear some back-and-forth in the background. "Hey, honey," his mom's voice came through the receiver after a minute. "How're you doin'?"

He could tell by the slight slur in her voice that she'd already gotten into the spiced rum. "I'm okay Mom. I'm up at Butterfly Lake, playing a gig tonight."

"That's nice, honey. I love when you sing. Can you sing me a song?"

Everett closed his eyes and took a steadying breath in. "I just wanted to see when—if—there was anything going on for Christmas."

"Nothing special. We ordered in take-out and Jason's taking Kimberly to ride her new tricycle in the apartment hallway. But sure, honey, you know you're welcome here anytime." He heard her take a puff of her cigarette. Actually, he *didn't* know that. His mom would be happy to see him. But whatever low life hanging around at her place never was.

"I'll come by sometime in the next few days. It would be great to see you." He glanced up at the wall, taking in the photos of Jeannie's family. A Canada Day barbecue. What looked like a fundraiser at a ski hill or something. A younger Duke with his arm around Sue in front of the lake, both of them tanned and grinning. Every wholesome, happy picture had the Carmichael family members smiling, arm-in-arm, like in some kind of cereal commercial.

"Hey, you heard from Jessie?" he asked, taking a chance. His mom and sister weren't always on good terms. His mom didn't believe there was anything wrong with her daughter beyond what she considered laziness for not leaving the house, as though his mother were some kind of model of excellent health herself.

"Not since she skipped Charlene's wedding, no," his mom said. "Cost them an arm and a leg for catering, and Jessie just plain doesn't show up. It was rude!"

Everett paused. "Go easy on her, okay, Mom? Things are tough for her." His sister went for long stretches of time not leaving her apartment, and when she did she got anxious and upset and panicked in busy public places.

"They're tough for everyone, sweetie. 'Cept maybe for you. My Golden Boy."

Everett heard Jason yell something. "Sounds like you've gotta go, Mom," he said. "Merry Christmas."

"Merry Christmas, baby. Love you lots."

"Love you too, Mom." He hung up the phone and slumped back in the chair. Maybe he'd call Jessie. But she wouldn't pick up. He'd have to go see her.

It was almost showtime, anyway. And he'd promised the Carmichaels a good time.

Before leaving the office, Everett leaned in to look more closely at Jeannie's photo, warming slightly at the sight of her easy, carefree smile. He felt desire, yes; there was no denying that. But was something more. He'd known the woman for less than forty-eight hours and found himself in the strangest way unable to picture life without her.

At the pub, Jeannie had been making eyes at the smarmy loser whom Everett had seen hitting on a different girl every night, either a member of the staff or a pub patron. The guy was all country club and trust fund, with a fresh haircut and brand-new loafers to match. If that were her type, he had no chance.

The truth was Everett could give her that life, twice over.

After graduating with his master's degree in natural sciences from the University of Calgary, he'd met an educational publisher at a conference, and they'd hit it off. The series of high school science textbooks he'd written for the publisher and sold over the past five years to every school in the province had put enough money in his bank account to last him a good long time, and the publisher wanted more, to align with the other provinces' curriculums. With a few tweaks here or there, he'd be in the hands of every biology, chemistry, and physics student in the entire country, to the tune of hundreds of thousands of dollars. They were also asking him to propose some ideas for a series of nature guides which would be sold at regular bookstores. But he didn't want Jeannie to know all this. Not yet.

He was taking a break between contracts, and for now playing in a band with his buddies was just good plain fun.

If he were ever lucky enough to get Jeannie Carmichael to agree to go on a date, he wanted it to be about *him* and not about what was in his bank account.

Chapter Five

IT WASN'T LONG after seven-thirty that the party was in full swing. The great room was packed with the Carmichael family, Duke and Sue's boarders, and fifty to sixty members of the Keystone Ridge community conversing, sampling all the delicious food, and admiring the giant Christmas tree that made the room come alive in a golden glow. Jeannie's second cousins, Lyndsay and Collin, had already made a dent in the dessert table, and Gloria was floating through the great room ensuring everyone had a beverage in hand.

The band was so good that there was already a dance floor, a new addition to the Carmichael Christmas Eve party.

The fact that Everett and his band were playing a mix of Billboard Hot 100 singles and upbeat Christmas songs didn't hurt either. The jazz trio had always been more of a background noise rather than the main event.

Right in the thick of things was Duke giving a bear hug to a guest who'd just arrived.

"Look who's here!" Duke said, turning to Jeannie with his arm around a man wearing a baby-blue turtleneck the same colour as his eyes and sporting a tidy blond side-part.

"Erik!" Jeannie said. "I hardly recognised you without the shaggy hair!" She hugged Erik Larsen, a former Aussie boarder who now lived in the city with his Canadian wife.

"I had to come, even for a few hours. But I had to leave Kristen behind," he said with a glint in his eyes. "Eight-and-a-half months pregnant. She's not up to travelling too much these days." He was dripping with pride and excitement.

"Send her my best," Jeannie said. "You'll have a January baby. They're always top of the class at school."

Duke practically ripped Erik's arm off, pulling him over to where Sue was holding court, and Jeannie stood alone again watching the band, sipping on a glass of white wine, and finding her gaze continuing to flicker back to Everett. He was very charming. Not really her type, but maybe one date wouldn't hurt. Being alone for New Year's was going to be depressing, especially given the fairy-tale evening she'd envisioned for that night.

When someone tapped her shoulder, she tensed up. It could only be one person. Sure enough, she turned to find Lincoln Morrison wearing a poorly fitting dress shirt and red tie, and looking just as much like the perpetual sad sack as she'd remembered. *He* was what her mother considered handsome? "Hi, Jeannie," Lincoln said, sliding his arm around her shoulder and looking her up and down. "You're looking great these days."

And you look like a used car salesman, she thought, forcing a smile. "Hi, Lincoln. What's new?"

"Not much. I've taken over managing the ski lodge. So, life's been good. You should stop by sometime." He raised his eyebrows and leaned in. "I'll hook you up with a free lift ticket." She instinctively shrugged her shoulder a little to loosen his grip as she caught a whiff of his unique brand of halitosis. A master pick-up artist.

"That sounds great, Lincoln. I'll have to do that." She rolled out from under his arm around her shoulder and took a step to the side.

"Wanna dance?" he asked. Jeannie glanced over to Everett and caught him observing the interaction intently. He raised his eyebrow, then turned back to the mic, where he added a harmony to the chorus of "Maggie May."

"I was actually just about to get another drink," Jeannie said, suddenly desperate to put more space between herself and Lincoln so that Everett didn't get the wrong idea. "Excuse me."

"I'll come with you," Lincoln said. *Ugh.* If only she hadn't been raised to be so polite.

With Lincoln on her tail, she shook her head as she approached the bar. What did she care if Everett thought she had a boyfriend?

"What can I get you?" asked Sam Forrester, the bartender from The Loose Moose in town, which was shut down for the evening since everyone who was out would be at the party. Sue had offered him the job, promising to put out a big and obvious tip jar knowing that he needed the tips these days, especially with twins on the way.

"I'll take a beer," Jeannie said to Sam, then turned back to face the stage while Lincoln ordered a beer for himself. Everett was confident and talented. She loved watching him play, and it was obvious she wasn't the only person in the room who felt that way judging by how many people were giving their full attention to the stage. She tried to divide her own attention evenly between the four members of the band, but she kept drifting back to him. Everett, on the other hand, was less concerned about being caught watching her. She drank in the feeling of his rapt attention.

"How about that dance?" Lincoln asked as soon as they both had their drinks in hand. Jeannie took a deep breath. She would give him one dance to get him off her case and to placate her mother, who was shooting daggers at her from across the room. Since they were holding their drinks, she could get away with not touching him.

Just as a song ended and the band played the opening notes of a slow Bee Gees song, Jeannie noticed out of the corner of her eye as Everett signalled something to the drummer, who appeared confused for a second. The song ended abruptly, and seconds later they launched into "Macho Man" by the Village People.

Jeannie almost burst out laughing, while Lincoln's face fell. "Aw, I liked that song," he said, but followed Jeannie's lead as she started dancing. She positioned herself so she could see the stage over Lincoln's shoulder and feigned interest in what he was saying—something about a new car he was planning to buy after the winter—while she continued to enjoy watching Everett play. They were no longer pretending they weren't purposefully making eye contact. She was happy she'd chosen the red sequins over the dowdy pinafore. Jeannie felt attractive and desirable, and wished it were Everett out on the dance floor with her instead of Stinky Linky.

The song ended, and Lincoln put both of their empty bottles on one of the tall circular tables bordering the room. Sue stepped onto the dance floor and took Jeannie by the elbow. "I'm so sorry to interrupt you two, but I need Jeannie's help in the kitchen," Sue said.

"Of course, Mrs. Carmichael," Lincoln said.

Bless you! Jeannie thought as she trailed Sue through the crowd. Once they were safely away from Lincoln, Sue turned and gave her a quick conspiratorial wink.

"I can't stand the thought of that snively little wimp thinking he has a chance with you," Sue whispered as they retreated into the kitchen. "But I do need your help. I completely forgot to put out the mulled wine. It's too hot to serve, though. Can you help me bring it outside to cool off for a couple of minutes?"

"Of course," Jeannie said. She accepted the oven mitts Sue passed her, then stood beside the pot waiting until her grandma was ready to lift. The mulled wine smelled like a holiday-infused dream, with cardamom, cinnamon, nutmeg, and orange peels floating at the top of the deep ruby-red drink.

"Careful, careful," Sue said. "Let's go out the side door."

Slowly, so nothing sloshed over the side and burned them, they carried out the steaming pot to the side of the lodge where it wasn't in danger of anyone stepping on it and placed it in a snow drift just off to the side of the stairs, using a tea towel as a cover to keep out the snow. It was so hot that the snow surrounding the pot melted instantly.

"I'll set a mental timer," Sue said. "Won't take much longer than ten minutes."

A strong wind blew a gust of flurries right into their faces. "Geez Louise! It's really coming down out here!"

Jeannie used her oven mitt to shield her face from the snow as they retreated back inside. It was almost a blizzard.

Back in the safety of the kitchen, they stomped their boots and shook the snow off their clothes. "I didn't realise we were getting a storm," Jeannie said. The forecast that day had called for light flurries, and nothing more.

"You know what it's like around here," Sue said. "Four seasons in one day, and a fifth if you're unlucky. Now, go on back out there."

"Just let me know when you want to bring that pot back in," Jeannie said.

"Say," said Sue. "I don't usually like loud music. But I like this band. Especially the guitar player," she said, winking at Jeannie. "He's a real sweetie."

Jeannie rolled her eyes. "Okay, okay."

"Any song you'd like him to sing?"

Jeannie's jaw dropped. Had Everett already gotten to her grandma?

He was persistent; she'd give him that.

AS SOON AS she returned to the great room, Jeannie ran right into her grandfather. His cheeks were rosy, and his plate was piled high with macaroni and cheese. Her heart warmed, seeing him enjoying himself so much. "Where's your grandma? Everyone's looking for her."

"She's right behind me," Jeannie said.

"Apparently there's some kind of surprise for her."

Duke spotted Sue coming out of the kitchen and waved her over. "The boys have something for you," he said.

"What the heck does that mean?" Sue asked. "You mean their rent for the month? Half of them still owe me for November! How am I supposed to winter next year in Tahiti at this rate?"

Jeannie smiled. Sue feigned annoyance at her boarders all the time, but she knew her grandma had a soft spot for them, and there was never a year where they weren't all paid up by the end of the season once they'd learned how to manage their money and not blow a whole paycheque at The

Grizzly House disco in Banff, where they'd been known to drink gallons of beer and order Chinese food through a hole in the wall between the bar and the restaurant, then stumble back into the lodge at what Sue called *ungodly hours*. Jeannie knew her grandma never slept deeply until they were all home and accounted for.

Jeannie watched as Phil, a twenty-one-year-old return visitor and one of the most spirited of the boarders, approached the stage with a glint of mischief in his eye and had a few words with Everett. Whatever he'd said made Everett smile, and after conferring with his bandmates, Everett passed Phil the microphone as Archie pulled a chair out to the middle of the dance floor, shooing the guests to form a circle around the periphery.

"Ah, hello everyone!" Phil said. "I'm Phil. I'm one of the lucky fellas who gets to live here for the winter with the Carmichaels, the best darn hosts you could ever imagine. So, the bunch of us have gotten together to prepare a little song for the woman who takes care of us all and puts up with us whackers!"

The crowd cheered, and Jeannie watched as Sue sat in the chair in the middle of the floor, grinning from ear to ear. "Someone's got to keep you bunch in line!" she called.

One of the other Aussies whistled loudly, then pulled a Santa hat from his back pocket and settled it on his thick mop of black hair.

One by one, all the boarders assembled at the front of

the room wearing matching hats, many of their shirts undone some or part of the way, two of the more muscular of the crew having lost them completely, eager to show off their sculpted physiques. Most of them were holding a pint or a beer bottle, a couple of them stumbling and a little more red-cheeked than the others.

"This one goes out to you, Mrs. Carmichael," Phil announced. "Or should I say, Mrs. Claus!" There were a few titters and murmurs from the crowd as Phil nodded to the band, who played the opening notes of Nat King Cole's "Mrs. Santa Claus." The crowd cheered, and Sue clapped as, one by one, each member of the group took to the mic and sang a line of the song with their own revised lyrics before passing it on to the next guy.

Who feeds the Aussies three times a day?
Who wraps our lunch and makes it gourmet?

Jeannie grinned and clapped her hands, as Sue bent over in her chair, laughing.

Who's helping us survive the workday?
Mrs. Santa Claus!
Who keeps our ski suits looking nice?
Who do we turn to for advice?
Who gives the brownies all their spice?
Mrs. Santa Claus!

The crowd was eating it up. The boarders crowded around the mic and sang the next section in unison.

She pitter-patters all around the kitchen
The whole year long
Amid the happy clatter of the kitchen
She scolds us all when we've done something wrong!

Sue was laughing so hard, tears streamed down her face, and the whole crowd was cheering on the boarders' terrible but endearing singing, if it could have even been called that. Wild applause roared at the end, and Jeannie gasped as the whole group of them surrounded her grandmother, hoisting up her chair and lifting her up above the crowd.

There were hugs all around after Sue was back safely on the ground. Jeannie looked over at Everett, who was smiling that delicious half-smile and playing a few chords on his guitar. "We're going to take a quick break," he said into the mic, and from the back of the room, Duke cued up a record to keep the music flowing.

JEANNIE PRETENDED NOT to notice as Everett wove his way through the crowd to her, and she smoothed out her hair quickly as she looked intently at her beer bottle.

"Is that guy your boyfriend?" he asked as soon as he was beside her. She was surprised by his directness and thrilled that he seemed to care.

"No. He's most definitely not my boyfriend." Thankfully *that* was cleared up.

"Good. Because I've been waiting to dance with you all night."

She barely had time to put her bottle down when, without another word, he took her hand and led her right into the middle of the dance floor and slipped his arm around her waist. She was already warm, but he was warmer, and the heat of electricity coursed through her body. She couldn't imagine how she'd almost not invited Everett and his band to play. It was a perfect night, and a perfect moment. She could have fun on Christmas Eve, couldn't she? Ben Kane wasn't the only one who could have a fling with someone from a pub.

"This has been a great night," Everett said, his warm breath tickling the fine hairs on her neck.

"I'm glad," she said. "I would have thought you'd have plans on Christmas Eve, though."

"Nothing as fun as this. This place is right out of a movie," he said. "And your family is great."

Jeannie glanced over first to her parents, who were talking to Mayor Kelley and his wife, then to Lyndsay and Collin, who were now fully sugared up and were chasing each other through the partygoers. Her mother caught her eye again, and the daggers had turned to lightning bolts. Gloria was *not* okay with a musician match-up; that much was clear.

Her mother might have been disapproving of Jeannie's outfit, but Jeannie knew Gloria was thrilled with the type of men that Jeannie met through her career. Men like Ben Kane.

"Yeah, they're all right," she said to Everett. If not a tad overbearing and a hint controlling—at least her mother. But she knew she was lucky.

"So… Which songs have you liked?"

"Hah. I'm not telling."

"You perked up during Chicago. Is it a Chicago song?"

"Nope."

"I thought I saw you sing along to AC/DC. Warmer or colder?"

"I'm not telling!" This was fun. Although there was a chance that he was just a giant flirt and he pulled this shtick with women at gigs all the time. "And are you stalking me or something? You should be paying attention to the party."

"Oh, I am," he said, pulling her a bit closer. "So, what you're saying is that we haven't played it yet?"

Jeannie shrugged. "Not yet," she said.

"We're running out of time. Can't I have just one clue?"

Jeannie bit her lip. "Fine. It has the word *love* in it."

Everett narrowed his eyes. He was even more irresistible when he feigned annoyance. "So, like every song."

"Not every one."

"You think I'm going to give up." He used the pad of his

thumb to trace a circle on the palm of her hand, and she was melting as quickly as the ice in Sam's bar bucket. "All right. I'm going to get some water, then we're back on stage," he said.

"Already?" asked Jeannie. *Don't leave*, she thought.

"That's why you're paying us the big bucks. Thanks for the dance." He pulled her hand up to his mouth and kissed it, his eyes alight with desire. "One more hint?" he asked.

"Get back on stage," she said, swatting him away. She couldn't wait until the next break.

"Just thought I'd try," he said, and then she was standing alone again, wondering if there was something about Christmas Eve that was making them all just a little bit loony.

Chapter Six

THE BAND CONTINUED to play hit after hit, and the number of guests on the dance floor grew. The air in the room was hot even though no one was tending to the fire which had started to dwindle.

And while her dress left a lot of skin exposed, Jeannie was overheating. Judging from how the other women were fanning themselves and how the men had shaken off their jackets, it was clear that the room needed some fresh air.

She wove her way through the crowd to the double doors that opened onto the patio and propped them both open. A blessedly cool breeze flowed in, the awning preventing the falling snow from entering.

Jeannie took some breaths of fresh air. She needed water. She'd already had a glass of wine and two beers, and didn't want to spend Christmas morning nursing a hangover.

At the bar, Sam was still busy doling out drinks, his tip jar filled with a healthy contribution from the community.

She drew in a few long sips of ice water from the glass Sam handed her and noticed Lincoln making her way toward her again. Oh good god. Would her grandma save her again?

She scanned the room for Sue just as the sound of a high-pitched squeal filled the air.

Jeannie searched for the source of the panic. Audrey Devlin, the third-grade teacher at the local elementary school, was looking toward the door Jeannie had just opened with a look of terror in her eyes, but the giant Christmas tree was blocking Jeannie's view.

In seconds, the music came to an abrupt stop, and just as Jeannie looked over to see the drummer staring gape-mouthed at the other side of the room, another yelp came from the dance floor, followed by a heightened murmur of concern. Jeannie moved to where she could see the back door and followed the drummer's gaze, then gasped.

Poking through the doorway, then slowly entering the room, were the antlers, and then the giant head and torso, of an elk, his snout dipped as he sauntered lazily onto the dance floor.

Partygoers scrambled to put as much distance between themselves and the beast. The sound of feedback came out of the speakers as the musicians dropped their instruments and the animal's snuff echoed from the ceiling.

"Crikey!" exclaimed Archie from beside the stage, his eyes wide.

"I think it's eyeing the profiteroles!" called Erik.

The elk took a few more steps forward, clumsily, with its eyes half-closed. Was it rabid? Could elk get rabies?

Partygoers raced by her toward the kitchen, but Jeannie

took a step forward and squinted, shaking off Lincoln's grip on her shoulder. She knew elks' snouts were dark, but this one seemed to have a pronounced ring around it. All the fur was stained dark purple, like a toddler who had just tried on his mom's lipstick for the first time.

"Holy jumping! The mulled wine!" Sue exclaimed. "He must have gotten into it!"

With all the excitement from the Aussies' song and dance, neither Jeannie nor Sue had remembered to bring in the pot. Judging by the lazily moving elk, who in any other circumstance would have stayed as far away from a raucous human party as possible, it did indeed look as though the beast has slurped its way through the entire vat of mulled wine, which must have contained at least twelve bottles of red wine.

"By golly, Blitzen's blitzed!" breathed Duke.

On stage, the drummer stared at his beer bottle as though it were laced with some kind of hallucinogen.

"Nobody make any sudden moves," Jeannie heard from the stage. Everett cautiously stepped down from the platform and made his way through the thinned-out crowd toward the elk, his hands raised as though he were approaching a volatile criminal and needed to prove that he wasn't carrying a gun.

At this point, the antlers were the most troubling. Jeannie had heard stories of aggressive elk charging and pushing vehicles right off the road.

She moved toward where Everett was standing.

"Jeannie, get away from there!" her mother hissed from the other side of the room.

She stayed planted next to Everett. "We just need to lure him back outside," he said quietly.

Without breaking eye contact with the beast, whose expression was now even more droopy, Everett plucked a sandwich off that someone had discarded before fleeing, then removed the piece of lettuce from it.

He continued to cautiously approach where the elk was standing. Jeannie's heart raced. If the elk charged, someone would be seriously injured. Or worse.

"Don't move, anyone," Everett said, his voice steady and calm. But there were only a few people left in the room. There was something in his self-assuredness and steady voice, though, that gave Jeannie confidence that Everett could solve their problem.

An obnoxious snarl sounded from over near the fireplace. Jeannie turned and saw Lincoln, who had grabbed the fire poker and was making a move toward the elk, waving the iron rod at it. He looked like a child playing with a lightsabre.

The animal didn't see Lincoln through the same rolled eyes the rest of the people did, and it flicked its ears back. It stomped its front hoof and let out a loud, watery huff. Jeannie froze in place.

"Drop that," growled Everett under his breath. "It's already confused. You're going to make him charge. Everyone else clear the room," he said, but anyone who hadn't already escaped to the kitchen, where Duke was holding the door open, was here to see this through.

Lincoln took another step forward. "What do you know about wild animals?" he asked, his eyes darting between Everett and the elk. "I've lived here my whole life. You're just a city boy wannabe musician."

At that point, Jeannie would have been happy for the elk to have picked Lincoln up in its antlers and carried him far, far away into the woods. If she were Everett, she might have clocked him.

Everett's eyes glanced from the elk to Jeannie. He needed her help. She gave him a quick nod, and then put her hand on Lincoln's shoulder, turning him to face her. She looked up at him with doe eyes. "I really don't want you getting hurt," she said, and at her words, Lincoln lowered the fire poker a bit, but continued to glare at Everett. "Please?" she asked, turning his chin now with her finger and gazing up at him, giving him permission to abandon his knight-in-shining-armor routine because she wanted, *needed*, him in one piece.

Lincoln brought his arm down, and she gave him a quick hug, watching over his shoulder and holding her breath as Everett placed one hand on the elk's face and the other on its strong wide torso and gently pushed it until it started to turn toward the door. She pulled back from Lincoln as soon as she felt it was safe.

"Come on, buddy," Everett murmured, then pulled the piece of lettuce from his pocket and dangled it in front of the elk's wine-stained snout. The elk took a tentative step toward the door. Everett continued to walk backward slowly, the giant creature sniffing and following him.

"Jeannie!" Sue hissed from the kitchen entrance. "Get over here!"

She glanced over quickly at her grandmother, then continued to watch as the elk made its way back outside, aided by its guide.

"At least it's not an angry drunk," Duke said.

She watched the empty doorframe, still barely able to breathe. What if the elk trampled Everett? Or lashed out with its hooves? Wildlife was unpredictable, and Jeannie imagined even more so when it was three sheets to the wind.

After what felt like an eternity, Everett slipped back into the room, eyes wide with a mix of disbelief and excitement. He slammed the double doors shut.

Jeannie exhaled.

"He did it!" Grandpa shouted back into the kitchen packed with party guests. A cheer erupted, and moments later Everett was surrounded by the few remaining guests shaking his hand and giving him high fives.

Lincoln glowered from the corner. Was he aware he'd just fallen victim to the distraction technique, the oldest trick in the book?

"A party to remember!" Sue said. "I don't know how I'm

going to sleep after that, but I'm going to bed!"

The back door swung open again, and a few cries erupted before everyone realised it was Constable McMurtry, the RCMP officer stationed at the detachment right outside of town. He dusted the snow off his crimson jacket and black-and-gold cap, and he kicked his boots lightly on the door frame before entering, then waved to the group.

"Are you here to escort our new friend to the drunk tank?" asked Duke.

McMurtry paused and cocked an eyebrow. "What now, Duke?"

"Never mind," said Sue. "Come in. Can we get you something to eat?"

"Not me," McMurtry said, glancing over his shoulder out the door he'd just come through, where the snow continued to fall. "Just came by to tell you all it's getting bad out there. County's closed the highways as a precaution. Anyone who drove needs to leave their car here tonight. If you're parked on the street, not to worry, no one's getting towed. But best be getting on home safely before it gets worse."

By then, the only neighbours who hadn't fled were the Sunderlands, who lived across the way and a few doors down; Mr. Garrison, who travelled exclusively by cross-country skis, so he'd be fine getting to his cottage a few minutes outside of town; and Erik, who appeared panicked.

"Highway's closed?" asked Erik. "But I promised my wife

I'd be home by midnight. She's going to kill me!"

Sue looked at Erik, and then at the band members, who were just as stranded as Erik. "Nothing to do now but stay overnight. We've got a few vacant rooms. Just give me a couple minutes to make up some beds."

"Happy to take the couch if you need an extra bed," Archie offered.

"You can get up first thing and get on the road," Duke said. "Something tells me they're just being overcautious. Snowplows will be out all night, and you'll be home with your wife by the time she wakes up. Go on and give her a call and let her know where you are. That goes for all of you. On the plus side, you'll get the chance to try Sue's chocolate chip pancakes in the morning. You may never leave."

Officer McMurtry wished them all Merry Christmas and was on his way, and just like that, the community celebration turned into a last-minute sleepover party.

Jeannie swallowed a lump in her throat. It was hours before the party was meant to end. They hadn't even done the group photo, so their final party would be absent from Sue's collection of group photos from over the years.

Not to mention that the grand finale was cancelled. Duke's favourite part of the night was his "surprise" fireworks show down by the lake. As always, he was planning to excuse himself right before midnight, and guests could watch outside in their jackets before heading home or from the warmth of the great room through the windows. What did it matter now? The snow would have made the fireworks invisible anyway.

Jeannie helped her grandparents see out the rest of the guests (and choked out an empty promise to visit Lincoln at the ski resort), kissed her parents goodnight, then wandered back into the great room, where she kicked her heels off, then flopped on a couch. It was supposed to have been a perfect last Christmas Eve party, and now people were going to bed at ten o'clock with barely a dent in the dessert table. It wasn't supposed to end this way.

She stared up at the ceiling, wiggling her toes to get the blood flowing again.

"Any recommendations?" she heard from only meters away.

Jeannie sat up quickly and found Everett standing in the puzzle room, the alcove where Sue and Duke kept their collection of jigsaws and mystery books.

He was pulling paperbacks off the bookshelf one by one, examining the covers.

Jeannie shifted her bare feet to the ground and smoothed her dress. "That's a good one," she said, noting the cover of one of her favourite Raymond Chandler books. "Might keep you up, though."

"Not too tired yet." He looked over at her. "How about you?"

Jeannie couldn't suppress a wide yawn from escaping her mouth. "I'm wiped," she admitted. Maybe it wasn't such a bad thing that the party had been shut down early. "See you at breakfast?"

"Looking forward to it," Everett said. "Do I get the morning too? To guess?" A small smile played on his lips.

He was so handsome. And she liked his persistence. "Fi-ne," she said. "You can have until you leave. But only because it's Christmas and I'm feeling generous."

"Lucky me," said Everett. "All right. Sleep well tonight."

"Wait," Jeannie said. "How did you know what to do? You seemed so calm. Like you wrangle elk for a living or something."

Everett paused, fixing her in his gaze. "I could tell you had my back," he said.

Jeannie warmed at his words. Did he mean them? "All I did was keep another beast out of your way."

"I guess we make a good team, don't we?" He tucked the book under his arm, then extended his hand.

Jeannie accepted the handshake, the warm strength of his grip sending a shiver of pleasure through her body. She held on for a few seconds and looked up into his gorgeous chocolate eyes. "Well, you saved the night, that's for sure. It didn't really go as expected. But between that, and the music…" She trailed off. *You were the best part of the night*, she wanted to say.

"All in a day's work," Everett said. He held up the book. "Thanks for the recommendation. Goodnight."

"Goodnight," Jeannie echoed, her breathing quick and

shallow.

She stood in the middle of the great room until she heard the click of his door closing in the hallway, then lay back on the couch staring at the ceiling again, a tingling desire pulsing through her.

Her dream of the perfect party hadn't come true. But she was going to see Everett again on Christmas morning. And that made her smile.

Chapter Seven

EVERETT HADN'T EVEN made it past page one before dropping his book on the bedside table and drifting into a deep sleep. He would have slept even longer if not for the sun streaming through his window, shining even brighter with the reflection off the new snow.

Christmas Day.

When he rolled over in his small single bed under the thick felt blanket, he was treated to a postcard perfect vista through the window. The mountains were so close and stately across the lake it felt like he could reach out and touch the craggy peaks. The bonfires were going again in the area between the lodge and the lake, and he could see Duke already down on the ice shovelling the rink, the ice sparkling in the sunlight.

Going back to the city and spending Christmas with his mom's lowlife boyfriend felt like a punishment now.

A faint knock sounded at his door. "Everett?" he heard Jeannie's voice call from the hallway.

He swung his legs out of bed and reached over to grab the t-shirt he'd slung on a chair and pulled it over his head.

He ran his hands through his hair, then cleared his throat. "Come in," he said.

The door opened, and Jeannie entered the room with a steaming yellow mug in her hand. "I brought you a coffee. Everyone's in the kitchen having breakfast. Merry Christmas, by the way."

"Thank you," he said. "Merry Christmas." He met her near the entrance of the room and accepted the mug. Waking up with a view of the Rocky Mountains in the sun? Being hand-delivered a hot coffee by the most beautiful woman he'd ever seen? Was he still in a hazy dream? This was a Christmas morning he could get behind.

Jeannie was back to casual in a pair of blue jeans and a black-and-red checkered sweater. Her hair was pulled back in a ponytail, her glossy lips every bit as inviting as they'd been in the great room before bed when he'd longed to kiss her goodnight.

"Did you sleep?" she asked.

"I did." He took a sip of the coffee. *Heaven.* "I can't get over this view. How much do these young guys pay to live here, anyway? I hope your grandparents are charging a premium."

Jeannie smiled. "They built the place where there wasn't a whole lot else in the area. Paid off the mortgage twenty years ago. So, they don't need to overcharge. They made a good investment."

"I'll say," said Everett.

The sun was out, and the sky was clear and blue. The fresh snow covered everything, but when he looked to the east of the building, he could see that someone had already been out to clear the snow off all the vehicles in the parking lot. The plows had been by too. "Looks like it'll be smooth sailing back to the city," he said. He took another sip of his coffee.

"Well, you can't get on the road without breakfast," Jeannie said. "See you down there?"

"I'm right behind you." But the last thing he wanted was to leave.

WHEN HE EMERGED from his room, the promise of chocolate chip pancakes wasn't looking so good. Patty, Kenneth, and Greg had already packed their bags and were waiting for him in the front foyer of the lodge. Sue was passing them cookie tins and bags of leftover sandwiches from the party, so at least there'd be something to eat on the trip home.

"Let's go, man," Greg said.

Everett tossed him the keys to the car. "You're driving this time," he said. He'd slept well but wanted to spend the first part of the drive gazing out the window.

He had to say goodbye to Jeannie before they left. "I'll be right back," he told the guys.

When he entered the kitchen, Jeannie was sitting at the

table with her father, and Erik was wiping his face with a napkin.

"I'm going to just call Kristen and let her know I'm on the way," Erik said. "A bang-up meal as always, Mrs. Carmichael!"

"It's been seven years, and I still have to tell you to call me Sue! Use the phone in the office. And tell your darling wife Merry Christmas and we apologise for the mountain weather."

Erik dropped his plate in the dishwasher and disappeared to the back office, while Jeannie's dad brought his plate to the oven for a second round of bacon.

Jeannie looked up at Everett from her breakfast. "Leaving already?" she asked. "What about breakfast?"

"The guys are ready to go, so…" Disappointment flashed in her eyes. "Maybe I should ditch the band next winter and get a job up—"

Everett stopped when the kitchen door swung open and Erik flew back into the kitchen in a panic. "She's in labour!" he yelled. "I've got to get in the car!"

"Wait, what?" Grandpa said. "She needs to get to the hospital!"

"She's there now! Her dad answered at the house! He was waiting for me to call. And he called me a downright slouch for not being there with her!" His eyes were wide with panic, his mouth agape.

They followed Erik outside as he all but leapt into his

car, mumbling something about thanks and goodbye.

"Now you drive safely," called Sue. "These babies take longer to come out than you might think. And that baby needs a father in one piece."

Erik nodded, gave a quick wave, and slammed his door.

They all watched from the porch as the engine of Erik's car sputtered, then cut out.

"Uh oh," Gloria said under her breath. "That's what you get for buying a foreign car."

"Mom!" Jeannie said, shooting her a look.

The engine chugged a little again, then died. And then a third time. Erik popped the hood of the car, then exited the vehicle, his eyes wild.

"I think it's the battery," said Jeannie's father, Jim.

"I'll get my jumper cables," Duke said.

Erik inspected under the hood, but it was clear he had no idea what he was looking for.

Within a few minutes, Grandpa's truck was connected to Erik's car and everyone was crossing their fingers that the engine would roar to life. But no luck.

"Not sure what's wrong with it," said Duke, "but why don't you take my truck?"

"I only know how to drive automatic!" cried Erik.

"You *what*?" said Grandpa. "Good lord, son, what kind of man doesn't know how to drive a stick?"

He looked back at the band, who were standing on the porch, bags in hand. "Any chance he can hitch a ride with you guys? Sue and I don't drive to the city. Haven't done it in over twenty years."

"Only if he can fit in the trailer," said Greg. "We can barely fit the four of us."

Everett felt for the panicked soon-to-be-dad. Erik had to be there for the birth of his child. "Guys," he said, and motioned to the group to come closer. "One of us should stay back. Give up a spot in the car. We'll call CAA and drive his car back to the city once it's fixed."

"It's Christmas Day. They'll take forever," said Greg.

"I'm not staying," said Kenneth. "My mom'll have my head if I'm not there for Christmas dinner."

"I'll stay," said Everett. He'd pull another something off the shelf of books in the library while he waited for CAA, the roadside assistance company, to arrive. It wasn't like he was dying to get back to spend Christmas dinner with his mom and Jason anyway, and it only took one look at the distraught expression on Erik's face for him to make his decision.

"All right, man, let's roll," Patty said.

With Erik in the back seat of the Gremlin, Greg navigated the car and trailer down the driveway, and Everett was left standing on the porch of the lodge with someone else's family.

"I'll go call CAA," Sue said, and disappeared to the back office.

"Come on in, son," Duke said. "We're going to exchange

gifts. I'm sure we can rustle something up for you. Right, Jeannie?"

Jeannie was looking at him with curiosity, a light smile on her pink lips. "You deserve a gift for giving up your ride like that."

"Oh, no need," said Everett. The last thing in the world he wanted was to sit and watch as the world's happiest family made each other even happier. He wasn't sure he'd survive it. "I didn't sleep too well, actually. If it's all the same to you, I might go back to bed for just a few minutes."

"Suit yourself," said Duke. "But there's no missing the Keystone Ridge Christmas Classic." He looked Everett up and down. "And you look like you can handle a puck! I call you for team Carmichael."

Everett glanced over at Jeannie again, who was now looking at him with an expression he couldn't decipher. Satisfaction? Amusement?

"*Brr!* It's as cold as a witch's teat out here. Get inside," Duke said, shooing them all in.

Chapter Eight

JEANNIE EXCUSED HERSELF to the washroom before gift opening began. She couldn't believe what had just happened. Everett McCarthy was going to spend part of Christmas Day with her family.

Thank goodness he'd excused himself from the gift exchange. Lord only knew what he'd think about the Carpenters record she'd gotten her mother or the traditional matching fleece pyjama sets she knew her grandparents had wrapped up for them all. She loved the gift exchange and didn't want anything to ruin it.

But…it was undeniably sweet the way he'd helped Erik, seemingly without a second thought. She liked to think she could be as selfless, but the idea of missing Christmas Day with her family was a dealbreaker. Didn't he have his own family to go home to? It was strange that he didn't seem too broken up about it.

When she exited the bathroom, Archie and Finn were on their way out the front door for their Christmas Day shift, and Everett had already disappeared back into his room.

"Left a message for CAA," Sue said. "Hope they'll be

quick!"

Jeannie followed her grandmother down the hall, glancing back at the door to Everett's room. Did he really want to be alone on Christmas morning, or should she invite him out again? She hesitated for a moment, then went to join her family. Who knew, maybe Christmas wasn't a great time of year for him. She'd give him space.

AN HOUR LATER, the Carmichael family was sitting amidst a sea of wrapping paper and a tower of things that no one really needed but had been delighted to open. Jeannie's favourite gift was a Polaroid camera from her parents, and she'd loved the expression on her dad's face when he'd opened the pocket calculator she'd bought for him.

"All right, who's ready to kick some Larson Family butt?" asked Jim. Everyone involved took this tournament just as seriously as if it were pro hockey.

"Why don't you go and see if Everett will come play?" Duke asked Jeannie.

Jeannie was still hesitant. According to Sue, it would likely be late afternoon at the earliest before CAA would be able to make it out to Keystone Ridge. Everett had been locked in his room all morning. But she couldn't deny that he appeared potentially athletic, and after the disastrous end to the party, she wanted the win for her grandpa.

"Fine," said Jeannie.

She left the great room and knocked on Everett's door.

"Come in," she heard, and slowly opened the door, peeking in to find him lying on the bed with his head propped up by pillows, legs crossed in front of him, and holding a different book than the one he'd picked out the night before.

"How's that one?" Jeannie asked.

"I've read it a bunch of times. But I still love it." He dog-eared the page, which made her bristle. She hated when people didn't use a bookmark.

Everett swung his legs over the side of the bed. "So, did Santa bring you everything you asked for? An argyle sweater? Pocket protector? Pet Rock?

She felt her cheeks go warm. "I got some nice gifts, yes." She straightened her shoulders. "You should come out and play. In the hockey game. It's a lot of fun."

"Are you playing?" he asked.

"No. I'll be scorekeeping."

"Of course," said Everett. "I'd have guessed that, or referee. Ever the commitment to law and order."

"Very funny," said Jeannie. "You'll be on team Carmichael, of course. Which means you're playing for the good guys. Which also means win at all costs."

"Good to know," said Everett. "I've never been much of a goon. But I'll do my best." He nodded to the side table. "I guess your grandma left those there for a reason."

On the table beside the bed was a tidy pile with a folded

jersey, and a crewneck sweatshirt to wear underneath, with the logo of the local Royal Canadian Legion emblazoned on the front. Everett pulled off his knitted sweater, revealing a long, lean, and sculpted upper body, not overly muscular, but clearly he did more than just play guitar. Jeannie's pulse quickened slightly, and she tried not to stare. Everett turned to look at her, his expression playful. "You're cheering for me though, right?"

She steeled herself, then backed out of the doorway. "See you out there," she said, almost slamming the door behind her.

EVERETT CHUCKLED TO himself, loving Jeannie's reaction to his outfit change.

Spending a few hours out on the ice might actually be kind of fun. It had been a few years since he'd last played a game of drop-in shinny at the university rec centre in between lectures, papers, and Thursday nights at McSorley's pub with his classmates. He'd be rusty, but that was okay.

He pulled on his jeans and the toque he'd been smart enough to shove in his coat pocket yesterday and checked his appearance in the mirror before going to join the world's most functional family down at the lake.

Hearing them opening presents—the laughter, the exclamations of gratitude, the affirmations that someone had picked out *the perfect gift*—he'd hardly been able to make it through more than four pages of his book. He felt more than a tinge of jealousy, but mostly longing. He'd had that once, when his dad was alive. And he missed it, a great deal.

THE RINK WAS freshly shovelled in a wide rectangle, the far side lined with benches made from overturned buckets and long wooden planks set into the snowbanks. The two teams had assembled down at the ice, a ragtag collection of players of all ages wearing their distinct jerseys of yellow or blue.

Everett grinned when he saw Sue skating some warm-up laps wearing figure skates and holding a hockey stick. "Don't you look at me like that," she yelled as he approached the edge of the rink. "I might look like a lady, but you don't want to mess with me!" She was moving pretty well for her age and had a great sense of humour. In fact, Everett loved her.

He crossed the rink carefully in his boots, sliding a little to avoid falling, then sat at the end of the bench and shook off his gloves to lace up his loaner skates. They were a little roomy.

As he tugged on the yellow laces, a memory flashed in his mind of his dad kneeling in front of him on the ice rink he flooded in the backyard for Everett to practice on. He'd blow on his bare hands to warm them up in between lacing up and tightening Everett's right and left skates, then he'd stand at the side of the rink to coach him, stomping his feet on the ice every so often to keep them from freezing.

Ronan McCarthy, who had moved to Canada from Ireland in his early teens after his own father accepted a teaching position at the University of Calgary, had never been a hockey player himself, but he wanted to give the experience to his son, given how popular the sport was in his adopted country.

Everett could remember his dad, an environmental engineer, bringing home a stack of books from the library and making notes about drills he wanted to teach his son. They'd spent hours out on the rink, and at the end of the practice, they'd sit and drink hot chocolate out of a thermos while Ronan told Everett all about how ice froze, how the temperature affected snowfall, and all sorts of other nature trivia.

Everett tugged the laces extra tight. He took a long, deep breath. What he wouldn't give to look up and see his father at the side of the rink again on this glorious Christmas Day.

He often dreamed about what it would be like to have him around. Sitting at the back of one of Everett's gigs, enjoying a pint of Guinness. Taking a day trip together to a hiking area. Calling him up to discuss the latest Premier League game.

When his dad died, Everett didn't just lose his father. He lost his whole family. His mom retreated into herself for the first few months, and then, as though she couldn't exist without a man by her side but couldn't be troubled to find a good one, the string of loser boyfriends started to appear in their lives. Jessie had already been an anxious child, and the disruption and unpredictability did such a number on her that she'd never really recovered. Everett felt like he was the only one who was holding it together, even though there had been many days he'd barely been able to fight through the sadness.

He looked up from his skates, watching as Jeannie and her mother set up the scoring table and Jim skated by, blowing kisses at his wife. Duke was carting equipment around, and Sue and Lyndsay were practicing passes. Did they know how lucky they were?

"Stick?" Everett heard. Duke was approaching him with an armful of options.

"What, you're not playing?" asked Everett. "I'd have figured you for the ringer."

Duke laughed. "Back in my time, maybe," he said. "They don't call me Rocket Richard for nothing. Haven't been able to skate since they put a new hip in me, though." He smacked his left side.

Everett selected a stick that seemed about the right size. "Well, I'm a little rusty myself. Wish me luck."

He pushed off from the bench and took some long strides forward to get his bearings.

The Carmichael team was made up of Sue; Jeannie's dad; Jacob, who didn't have a shift that day; and two of Jeannie's second cousins, ten-year-old Collin and a teenage girl named Lyndsay, who apparently was trying to get a new sport called ringette going in the area, but in the meantime was content to play what she called the *boys' game*. She was a terrific skater, and after a few minutes of warm up, she and Everett had established an easy pass system that could yield them some goals.

"Two minutes to puck drop!" Duke called.

Everett took the chance to skate by the scoring table. Jeannie was wearing a bright-green toque and a white jacket with a fur trim. She was organizing a pile of numbers for the flip chart in front of her. "Is there a prize for winning?" he asked.

She looked up. "Well, of course there's a prize."

Everett leaned on his stick. "A date? I'd like another chance."

She scoffed, but he knew from the slight grin she couldn't suppress that he was chipping away at her. "No, that's not the prize." But then her expression changed, and Everett turned to see Duke giving Sue a pep talk at the side of the rink. "Actually, fine," she said. "Since you failed at guessing my favourite dance-floor song."

"Is it a Kate Bush track? It's Kate Bush, isn't it?"

"No, not even close." She bit the corner of her bottom lip and dipped her chin a little so she was looking up at him with those bright, enchanting eyes. "It's 'I Feel Love' by Donna Summer. You want to get me on any dance floor, put that one on."

In that moment he knew he must really like Jeannie, because as far as he was concerned, Donna Summer could sing, but disco was trash. But the way Jeannie's eyes were sparkling made it easy for him to overlook her questionable taste in music.

"I suppose you haven't heard of the Carmichael Cup," she continued. "It's second only to the Stanley Cup in its degree of coveted-ness."

"Sounds serious."

"It is. And you bring home the cup—I'll go on a date with you."

"Clear your calendar," Everett said. The ref's whistle blew, and he left to join the rest of the players gathered around centre ice for face-off. Everett skated to his position, then looked back at Jeannie, her cheeks and nose flush from the cold. She was as gorgeous as ever, smiling as she gave him a thumbs-up.

He was going to win this game.

AFTER THE FIRST period, the Larsons were up two to nothing. The teams were fairly even in the players' skills, and those who knew how to handle the puck made sure that the less experienced players were included while at the same time engaging in some healthy competition with those who were more at their level. Everett found himself somewhere in the middle. He'd had a few good chances on net, but Cole Larson, who was built like a brick, was a decent goalie, if not for any notable reflexes and dexterity but for the sheer amount of space he blocked just by standing in the net.

The temperature had warmed up considerably since the morning, and with the sun shining right overhead, the ice had started to melt slightly, leaving a light slushy layer on the surface. They were all soaked, both from the ice and from sweat.

Jim brought them to within one goal at the beginning of the third period, and when Everett skated by the scoring table, Jeannie called out to him. "You told me you're a sniper!" she yelled, her eyes dancing with mischief. He'd be damned if he didn't win this game.

With just over three minutes to go, Everett called a time-out. He could still remember every detail his dad had taught him about the strategy for playing on wet ice. The team huddled around him, and he spoke quietly so his voice wouldn't carry.

"Their goalie is going down early, and by now his pads are wet and heavy, so pump fake, and when he goes down, bury it upstairs, preferably stick side," he whispered. "And keep passing—we want them skating as much as possible. It's more tiring to skate on the wet ice. Got it?"

"Got it," his teammates answered. After a quick team cheer, they skated back to take a face-off in the offensive end.

They played hard but smart for three minutes, moving the puck around as much as possible and keeping their passes short. As expected, the opposition was really winded, and finally they had to call a time-out to catch their breath.

"One minute remaining!" called Duke from the sidelines. Jeannie gave Everett another thumbs-up, and he looked over at Lyndsay and nodded. "Let's go," he said.

Shortly after play resumed, Everett saw his opening, and it was now or never. With a quick burst of speed, he swept past two yellow jerseys, and Lyndsay saucered a pass that landed right on the tape of his stick blade. Now in the clear and sweeping in on net, he glanced up at Cole, then faked a quick snapshot and, just as he'd hoped, the goalie immediately went down. Everett fired the puck at the top left corner with a powerful flick of his wrist, where for a heart-stopping moment he heard a familiar clang as the puck hit the crossbar before deflecting down into the net. Goal!

Seconds later, team Carmichael had surrounded Everett in a raucous huddle, and through the high fives and hugs, he strained to catch a glimpse at Jeannie. She had her arms up in the air and a huge grin on her face.

"You're a hero for the second time in twenty-four hours!" said Sue, wrapping her arm around Everett's shoulders. "Way to go, my boy!"

They were one goal away from tying, and two from him locking down a night out with his dream woman.

They skated hard; they executed passes; and Duke, Gloria, and Jeannie yelled like maniacs from the sidelines.

But it wasn't to be.

All three of their shots on goal within the last minute were deflected, and to add insult to injury, the opposing team scored with three seconds left in the game, earning a four-to-two victory.

The Larsons were presented with the Carmichael Cup, which was actually an oversized ornate beer stein from a trip Duke and Sue had taken to Scotland for their honeymoon over thirty years ago where they'd come across the vessel emblazoned with the family name. It had a Scottish bagpiper in traditional costume on the front, with dragons and castles and a large silver dagger decorating the rest of it.

Now, Duke told Everett, after every Christmas Day hockey tournament, the winning team was added to a paper on the inside, under the silver latched cover.

Graciously, the Larsons returned the cup to its rightful owner. "She's home again," Duke exclaimed, but Everett could tell by the slight downturn in Jeannie's eyes that even though it was a friendly game between families, she was disappointed they hadn't won.

Everett hated to lose.

But even more, he hated that he *still* didn't have a date with Jeannie Carmichael.

Chapter Nine

"IT WAS STILL a nice goal," Jeannie said as Everett approached the firepit with a bottle of beer in his gloved hand. It wasn't just nice. Jeannie knew she'd be hearing about that shot for years to come, Carmichael family lore right up there with the thirty-two-pound rainbow trout Duke had caught in the Bow River twenty years ago.

Remember that musician who got stranded at Christmas and ended up making the day's most heroic play? they'd say, voices thick with nostalgia. She wasn't sure what would get more airtime, the shot or the redirect of the Christmas Eve elk.

What stuck out to her, though, was how intent Everett had been on winning. He'd barely taken a second to celebrate before locking eyes with her across the rink. He was trying for *her*.

"It was a lot of fun," Everett said. "But I still can't believe we lost like that." His cheeks were bright pink and his hair was a bit wild from the wind now that it was free from his toque, which he'd shed. "Now tell me about what's going on here." He stood over the cast-iron pot hanging a safe distance above the fire, gooey white melted Emmental cheese bubbling lightly inside. On a table between the two firepits—the other with its own vat of cheese, that one Gruyère—was a table with paper plates, napkins, long metal spears, and an assortment of dippable items like cubes of cured meat, crudités, and cut-up apples and pears.

"What's going on here," Jeannie said, "is an obscene amount of cheese, with every possible item you would ever want to dip in it. But I'll let you in on a little secret."

Everett raised his eyebrows. "Finally, you're opening up to me," he said. She hoped the cold was hiding the blush in her cheeks. "I'm all ears."

Jeannie straightened her shoulders and looked at him pointedly. "The fondue is good. Very good. But go easy. Because tonight's meal is something dreams are made of, and it's a rookie mistake to load up too much on the fondue. You'll be too full for dinner, and you'll have to look on forlornly while the rest of us indulge in the finest Christmas Day dinner you've ever seen. Trust me."

"I'll be on the road by dinner, hopefully," Everett said.

"It's Christmas Day. I doubt roadside assistance will be on time," Jeannie said. She doubted, but mostly she hoped. Watching Everett play so hard to try to get her family the win… Maybe they'd lost, but she was smitten. "Trust me."

Everett speared a soft cube of French bread and dipped it carefully into the pot, then held it over a napkin in the crisp breeze to cool for a moment before taking a bite. Jeannie watched the predictable reaction: Everett groaned as his mouth filled with the flavour of rich, salty cheese. She could tell that in that moment he could think of nothing other than plopping himself in front of the fire until he'd scraped every last morsel from the cast-iron pot. "Oh wow. It's not going to be easy. But what you're saying is I should trust you."

"That's up to you to decide," Jeannie said, dipping a piece of pepperette directly into the pot and raising her eyebrows as she blew on it a little, then popped it in her mouth. "But don't make me say I told you so."

He plucked a cucumber from the platter, then paused, studying her. "You okay?" he asked.

"What do you mean? I'm fine."

"You seem a little down," he said. "Compared to earlier."

Jeannie paused. She didn't want to make him feel bad. Or judge her for what was probably a childish attachment to her family traditions. "It's just that things seem to keep going wrong. And this is our last Christmas here."

Everett turned to look at the lodge. "I heard something about that. Your grandparents are selling this place, right?"

"Yeah. So, this is the last hurrah for a lot of our traditions."

"I get it." He turned back to her, his brown eyes filled with warmth and care. "You wanted everything to be perfect."

"Exactly."

Over by the other bonfire, Duke was in the middle of telling an animated story to the Larsons. "Your grandfather doesn't seem too bothered by it. Maybe there's another version of perfect than the one that's been in your mind. Because I'll tell you. If this," he said, waving out at the vista in front of them, "and the party last night, and what you're saying is going to be a great family meal, isn't perfect, I don't know what is. You've gotta count your blessings, Jeannie Carmichael."

Jeannie opened her mouth to speak, but Sue was shouting something about a group photo on the rink, so she stayed quiet and let her grandmother corral the group for a shot.

AFTER THE FONDUE, the group sat in the wooden chairs and on makeshift stools from various items around the property. Jacob had clearly spent some time making his seat, a throne made out of snow, adorned with pinecones and twigs. It was all a bit silly, and Jeannie was a little embarrassed when it was her turn to take the "stage" for charades.

Everett told them he wasn't much of a games person and waved off an invitation to participate, then sat back and watched those participating mime *airplane*, *dream*, *lizard*, and *rainbow*.

Jeannie did her best when acting out *Frankenstein*. She

felt like she performed *unicycling* with particular aplomb, and absolutely aced *teapot.*

She found herself continuing to look at Everett, hoping he was enjoying himself and wanting to make sure he was okay. He thought her family, with all their quirks and flaws, was perfect. What was up with his?

BY FIVE O'CLOCK, roadside assistance was still nowhere to be seen, and Jeannie warmed at how her family made every effort to include Everett, even giving him his own Christmas cracker with a paper hat that he was instructed he needed to wear to the "Under the Sea" dinner. They were pretty amazing, she had to admit. It likely helped that he wasn't the only non-family member there, and he seemed to enjoy the banter of the Aussies, who had now all returned from their shifts at the ski resort.

Jeannie showed Everett to his seat at the table, across from hers and one seat over. "The 'Under the Sea' dinner title is no joke," she said. "Although, technically everything in the meal is very much no longer under the sea."

Everett's eyes widened as platters of shaved ice holding shucked oysters and every variety of mignonette and sauce as accoutrements, with wedges of lemon to drip over the top, were placed on the table. On a separate platter came some oysters that were baked Rockefeller-style, with butter, parsley, and breadcrumbs.

Duke served each seat a steaming bowl of lobster bisque in stoneware bowls. Jeannie grinned watching Everett blow on his a little before taking a bite, then groaning in pleasure. "Nothing in the world will ever live up to this soup," he said to Sue, who waved off the compliment but was clearly pleased.

There was blackened red snapper and pan-fried salmon with watercress sauce, and on the centre of the table was a five-tiered stand heavy with fat pink shrimp, spindly king crab legs, mussels, clams, scallops on the half shell, and dishes of chili sauce, brown butter with capers, and cocktail sauce.

When a plate of warm cornbread muffins and thick slabs of French bread came around, Everett tipped one of each onto his plate.

"Told you," Jeannie said. "Fondue was good…"

"But this is truly heaven," Everett said.

"Exactly," said Jeannie. She loved that Everett was having a great time. She sent a silent *thank you* to all the other Albertans who had made CAA calls today and were slowing down service, and mentally crossed her fingers he'd stay the rest of the evening.

"So, Everett," Duke said. "We know you can shred the guitar. Somehow you've got some kind of weird connection with animals, and you can handle a puck. Can't close, but you're okay." Everyone laughed. "So tell me, my boy, who's missing you tonight?"

Jeannie's jaw tightened when she noted the slight sloop of Everett's shoulders at Duke's question.

"Ah, my mom's in Calgary, actually, and my sister's in Cochrane." He took a sip from his water glass, his eyes fixed on his plate.

"And what are they doing to celeb—"

"Duke, don't be nosy!" Sue implored, swatting him with her paper napkin. "Now, Everett, tell us how you learned to be such a good hockey player."

Everett's eyes flickered to Jeannie, then back to his plate.

"Why don't we pop our Christmas crackers?" Jeannie asked loudly. She knew her interjection was awkward, but when Everett mouthed "Thanks" from across the table, she smiled back at him.

Crackers were popped, paper crowns adorned, and they all took turns reading out their fortunes from the small papers inside.

"'You will soon be travelling to a distant land,'" read Sue. "There you go, Duke. Time to book our plane tickets to Aruba for next winter."

"Ten-four," Duke said. He slid his glasses from his shirt pocket, then examined his fortune. "'As soon as you feel too old to do something, do it,'" he said. "Well, there's a fortune! Time to get me that Harley-Davidson I've had my eye on."

"There's enough roadkill in these parts, honey," Sue said, then kissed him on the cheek.

"'You will be awarded some great honor,'" read Jim.

"Best husband in the world," said Gloria, and slipped her arm around his shoulder. Jeannie rolled her eyes, but they were pretty cute.

She reached inside the ripped paper cylinder and unfolded the small piece of paper inside, then cleared her throat before speaking. "'If you want the rainbow, you have to tolerate the rain,'" Jeannie read aloud.

"And bring your umbrella," said Sue.

When Jeannie looked over at Everett, he was giving her a pointed look.

"What?" she mouthed to him while the rest of the table read their fortunes.

He shook his head and smiled. She was dying to know what he was thinking.

So, when a welcome break was announced between the meal and dessert, Jeannie looked across the table at Everett, with his completely empty plate in front of him. "Come to the great room," she said while the others were moving dishes and platters off the table.

She led through the great room to the puzzle room where they could have a few quiet moments.

"So, was I right, or was I right?" she asked, gesturing to Everett to sit at the table where she'd started a Wonder Woman puzzle the day she'd arrived.

"It's official. I trust you," he said, sitting back in a winged leather chair, letting out a contented sigh. "The fondue was incredible. But *that* was a meal."

Jeannie smiled to herself as she sorted through the remaining pieces of the mostly completed puzzle between them. Everett helped her by sifting through and pulling out the remaining edge pieces. "So, what was that look all about?" she asked.

"I don't know what you mean." He pressed in a corner piece.

"When I read out my fortune."

Everett's chin was dipped, but she could tell he was amused. He looked up, his deep-brown eyes alight with pleasure. "I just liked the way you read it," he said.

EVERETT HAD NEVER been so full in his life. He was happy to be taking a break from eating and to have some quiet time with Jeannie. He watched her as she scanned her puzzle, enjoying how she bit her lip just slightly while she sized up her piece and searched for its home.

"I'm sorry my family is so nosy," she said quietly. Her family had moved into the great room and while they were all talking animatedly, they were still within earshot. "They mean well. But small towns, you know."

"It's all right," Everett said. "It's just that if I gave honest answers to their questions, it might have dampened the mood a bit."

"I'm sorry."

"Stop apologizing. Your family is great. I've had a lot of fun today."

Jeannie paused. "You don't need to talk about it if you don't want to. But I'm interested in the honest answers."

Everett considered. It was just the two of them in a quiet room. There was a chance he may never see Jeannie again. What was the harm in telling her? "My dad taught me to play hockey. He died when I was ten. Things with my family haven't really been all that great since then."

Jeannie's face dropped. "I'm so sorry," she said. "I—"

"You don't have to be sorry. That's life. He was generally a really healthy guy but got Legionnaires' disease and died pretty quickly." The disease usually only killed people who were unhealthy, or with compromised immune systems. From diagnosis to his death, it had been just under two weeks, barely enough time to come to terms with what was happening and to figure out how to say goodbye. "To be honest, I kind of felt guilty celebrating anything without him after he died. It wasn't fair that his life was so short. So, that's why I haven't really been a Christmas person. But this," he said, gesturing through the doorway back toward the great room and the scene that was playing out there, Sue and Lyndsay painting with Lyndsay's new watercolour set, Archie, Jacob, Finn, and Jim playing euchre, and Duke arranging the logs in the fireplace, "is really nice."

"I know," Jeannie said softly. She reached across the table

and brushed his hand with hers, and the smoothness and warmth of her skin softened the ache in his heart.

The sun had dipped beyond the mountains, and the sky was a deep indigo, already punctuated by stars. Everett picked up one of the last few puzzle pieces and fit it neatly into place. "I guess I was always really angry with my mom for not being able to hold it together for us. She crumbled after my dad died. I wanted her to be stronger."

"Like you were?"

"I don't know about that. I could have been a better son." The second the words left his mouth, he felt a flash of guilt like a punch in the gut. Why had he put the onus on his mother to return their small family to some semblance of happiness? Sure, she'd been the adult, but certainly he'd had a role to play. "I was unfair to her." Everett picked up the last puzzle piece left on the table and placed it into the middle of the scene, but there were still a few empty spots. "Looks like we're missing a few pieces."

Jeannie peered under the table, then back in the box. "Ugh. That drives me crazy. I hate missing pieces. And after all the time putting it together." She looked up at Everett with an exasperated expression on her face. All he could do was smile. "What?" she asked, a wide grin creeping over her face.

Her annoyance was adorable, and he was tempted to push her further. "I've noticed you're a bit…" Everett paused.

"Just say it."

"You like things to be just so."

"What's wrong with having high standards?"

Everett looked at the puzzle, then up at Jeannie. "Nothing wrong with that. I guess I'm just more of a—" He searched for the right word, not wanting to insult her or ruin the moment. "I guess I've always been more okay with *perfectly imperfect*. You like the rainbow without the rain."

Jeannie's expression softened. "Feels like you're giving me some fodder for a New Year's resolution." She shifted the puzzle a bit on the table and smoothed the top so the pieces sat flush at the surface. "Maybe you'll patch things up," she said, studying his expression. "With your mother. I know it's not easy. But I'm sure she's missing you. She's your mom."

"You're right," Everett said. And she was. Jeannie wasn't just book smart, but from everything he'd observed—how loving and attentive she was with her grandparents, how she'd let that dude on the dance floor down easy—she was attuned to people's emotions as well. "But I don't want the rest of this day to be about me and my family drama." He glanced out the window. Time to change the subject. "I've seen them a million times, but I can never believe how bright the stars are out here."

"Agreed," said Jeannie. "They're amazing. And you have to make your Christmas wish now," she said.

"Is that another Carmichael family tradition?" Everett asked. "I'm having trouble keeping track of everything."

"No, that's new," said Jeannie.

"Okay," he said, sitting back in his chair and folding his hands in his lap. He closed his eyes. "I wish…for a lifetime supply of that lobster bisque." He opened his eyes and grinned. "Your grandmother is a wizard."

Jeannie swatted him. "Be serious!" she said. "And you can't tell your wish, or it won't come true."

"Fine," Everett said, and he closed his eyes and pretended to put something out into the universe.

But he'd already made his wish many times that day, every time he'd looked at Jeannie.

AFTER DESSERT—A DECADENT Bûche de Nöel topped with airy Chantilly cream—Everett stood up to help clear dishes but was immediately instructed to sit back down. "You're our guest," said Duke. "And you should be charging us overtime for how long you've had to stick around here."

"It's been my pleasure," Everett said. He hoped his words came across as sincerely as he meant them.

"At this point, you'd better just stay over again," said Sue. "No use driving this late at night."

Everett noticed Jeannie looking up from her seat.

"Why don't I call and get an updated ETA," Sue said, "and then how about you play us a couple songs, then, while we clean up? That'll make for fun work."

"Happy to. Any requests?" he asked Jeannie. "No Donna Summers."

"Ha. Fine," she said. "How about Gordon Lightfoot?"

"You've got it," said Everett. He retrieved his guitar from the front entrance and found a place by the fire. He capo'ed the guitar at fret two and started picking the opening to "Song for a Winter's Night," which seemed fitting. The family cleared the table and continued chatting amongst themselves, and Everett was happy to exist amid the din of the evening's noise rather than as the main event. He played Lightfoot; he played James Taylor, Joni, Elton, and Neil Young, and after a while, one by one, the Carmichaels drifted over to where he was sitting and settled onto the couch to watch him play. Jim joined in with Everett here and there, albeit a little off-key, and the boarders continued on with their euchre game.

"Bravo, bravo!" exclaimed Sue after he'd played the last notes of "Moonshadow." "You've sang for your supper now. CAA said there's still a big backlog after last night's storm. So, it's likely to be the morning. What can I get you to drink?"

He couldn't imagine putting another single thing in his body. "I might get some air, actually," he said. "Excuse me."

"Movie night starts soon," Sue said, tapping her watch. "Pyjamas are the dress code."

Everett grabbed his jacket from his room, then slipped out the front door onto the front porch. It was cold, quiet, and still. The fresh snow crunched under his boots on his way to the main road. He stopped at the end of the driveway and looked up at the tall sycamores and the stars dotting the night sky.

The last Christmas gift his dad had ever given him was an Edmund Scientific telescope. Everett had spent hours that winter peering through the viewfinder, his dad over his shoulder, instructing him in the different constellations visible at that time of year through the finder scope. "We'll go to Jasper in the summer," his dad had said. "It's one of the world's largest dark-sky preserves."

But his dad hadn't made it to that summer. The universe was vast, beautiful, and incredibly unfair.

It really, really wasn't fair. But Everett couldn't live the rest of his life yearning for what might have been.

A bright light in the sky caught his eye. It was a shooting star.

A sign.

He shivered as the breeze picked up, and he made his way back to the lodge. Through the front window, he saw Jeannie and her cousins bringing bowls of popcorn and chips out of the kitchen and placing them on the table, chatting and laughing and enjoying one another's company. He would have that again one day too. He would make sure of it.

Chapter Ten

WATCHING EVERETT PLAY guitar without his band made Jeannie melt into a puddle of gooey maple syrup. She knew he had a good voice, but hearing it on its own, with only his guitar and without the backup vocals or drums, was an irresistible treat. She could have listened to him play all night.

How could she have been so dismissive of him being a musician? It was obviously a true talent, and so what if he shared that talent at a corner pub instead of Carnegie Hall?

She felt a pang of remorse for looking down on him as though it weren't honest work and a respectable way to earn a living, especially given what he'd been through in his life.

While her family was busy getting changed for movie night, she slipped away and grabbed her jacket. She wanted more time alone with Everett.

Unfortunately, Duke was also outside enjoying his once-a-year cigar, and he and Everett were in conversation midway down the driveway. Jeannie stayed back in the shadow under the porch awning, listening quietly.

"What did you say your last name was?" asked Duke.

"McCarthy," Everett responded.

"Everett McCarthy," Duke said. "It's the darndest thing, but that name sounds familiar."

"Huh," Everett said. "Maybe you're prescient or something. You've been into the future when I'm a famous rock musician."

Duke chuckled, and Jeannie smiled to herself. He had the talent; that was for sure. And he definitely had the looks and charisma. But there was something private about him too, and Jeannie couldn't see him being someone to enjoy all the trappings of fame that came along with that.

The door swung open behind her, and Jeannie jumped. "What are you doing out here all alone?" Sue asked.

"Just getting a breath of fresh air," Jeannie said.

"Ugh," said Sue, waving the air in front of her and craning her neck to see where her husband was. "I hate it when he smokes these things. Duke! Erik's on the phone! He has some news he wants to share with you!" She looked at Jeannie. "Now get inside, you. We don't need you spending the rest of your vacation with a cold."

Jeannie followed Sue inside. "I saved you a seat here, honey, so you can rub my feet during the movie," Gloria called from the couch located in the den at the far end of the great room.

"Lucky me," Jeannie said.

She didn't want to watch the movie. She wanted to go back outside and find Everett, but didn't know how to get out of movie night.

A minute later, Grandpa returned to the great room. "It's a girl!" he shouted, and everyone cheered.

A Christmas baby. How lovely. So, the party hadn't gone as expected. They'd lost the game. But dinner had been excellent, and they had happy news to celebrate.

Everett's words about her family echoed in her mind. She was lucky. So what if not everything had gone according to plan? She would settle in with her family for the last big movie night at the lodge and be present with them.

By the time the movie ended, Jeannie still hadn't seen Everett return indoors. Had CAA arrived and fixed the car? She'd be surprised if he'd left without saying goodbye. Maybe he'd come through the side entrance and slipped into his room with no one noticing. It had been a lot of Carmichael time that day, so she wouldn't blame him, but Jeannie couldn't help but be a bit disappointed he hadn't even said goodnight.

After washing her face and brushing her teeth, Jeannie peered out her second-floor bedroom window. In the darkness, the only thing visible were the three firepits. Two of the three were smouldering, but it appeared as though the one closest to the lake was being stoked by someone sitting in front of the dancing flames. She squinted, trying to make out who it was.

Everett.

She checked her watch. It was almost midnight. Should

she go down and talk to him? Or did he want to be alone? Christmas was obviously a challenging time for him.

However, something in his eyes at the party the evening before—when she'd first entered the great room in her dress—as well as the current of electricity that had hung thick in the air hours earlier told her that he might welcome her company.

Jeannie slipped down the back staircase to the mudroom and pulled on her long down jacket, a toque, and her snow boots, then crept to the kitchen and poured the remnants of the apple cider from the standing carafe into a thermos. She grabbed two tin mugs, then quietly made her way out the back door.

The sound of her boots crunching through the snow alerted Everett to her presence.

"Well, look who it is," he said, his face lit up in the glow of the flames.

"How long have you been out here? It's freezing," she said. "I brought you some cider."

"It's comfortable by the fire," he said, gesturing to the seat beside him. "And look," he said. "We've got quite the show going."

Jeannie looked up to see the faint green glow of the aurora borealis, something she hadn't seen since she was a little girl.

She settled in the seat next to Everett and poured them both half a mug of cider, the cinnamon steam warming her face in the cold air.

"It's magic," Jeannie said. "Pure magic."

"Well, technically it's a solar wind that causes a stream of particles to penetrate the magnetic field of the earth, and those particles react with the gases in that field."

Jeannie shot him a look. "What's with you and all the science jargon?"

He grinned. "Sorry. We can go with *magic.*"

She examined his expression. "You were making that stuff up."

Everett held his glove-covered hand up in the air. "Scout's honor. And have you ever seen a Celestial Cascade? It's like the northern lights on steroids."

"I haven't. What's that?"

"Mother Nature's greatest light show. Happens very rarely, and under very specific conditions. The sky gets all pink-and-purple streaked, and stars twinkle brightly enough that even the light pollution in the city can't drown them out."

She liked how he could explain something without sounding like a know-it-all. "You sure know a lot about astronomy. You said you were a Scout?"

Everett nodded. "I spent my childhood outside. Canoe trips on the Nahanni. Hiking the Columbia Icefield. Camping in Haida Gwaii. My Dad was a real adventurer. He brought me everywhere."

"Huh," she said. "So, that's how you learned to wrangle giant angry animals?"

"I picked up a few things along the way."

The fire crackled and popped as Everett poked it with a long stick. It lit up his features, and for the first time, in the flashes of light and shadow, Jeannie noticed faint dimples at the sides of his mouth when he smiled. It was nice having this time with him, alone, away from her mother's prying eyes, without Lincoln hanging off her shoulder.

"So, what, are you going to sleep out here?" Jeannie asked. "It's getting late." She immediately wanted to take her words back in case he agreed and decided to retreat to his room. She felt both comfortable and nervous around him at the same time, like she'd known him forever, but cared a lot what he thought about her.

"We could," he said. Jeannie noted the *we*, and a shiver of pleasure ran through her. "Have you ever built a quinzhee?"

"A what?" she asked.

"It's kind of like an igloo, but you build a mound of snow and dig it out, with just a small hole to get in and out."

"No, and I think I'm okay with that. I'm more of an Egyptian sheets and electric blanket kind of gal myself." Which probably knocked her down a few pegs in his books, but there was no use pretending.

"Shame. It's a great experience. You'd have to stay close, though." His eyes flickered with mischief and desire. He was flirting with her. And she was lapping it up. "For warmth, I mean."

She was warm. And it wasn't just the crackling flames of the fire. She wished she had a witty quip, but instead she took a moment to indulge in the thought of Everett's arms around her keeping her warm, an idea that sent a surge of pleasure through her body. "Did you grow up outside of the city?" she asked, the inane question all she could manage.

He grinned as if he knew full well he was getting under her skin and was loving it. "Nah, we lived close to the university. But my dad took me out any chance he got," Everett said, a thin smile on his face. "I've always been tempted to move up this way, but there aren't too many gigs available."

"Have you ever thought about doing something else?" she asked. "I mean, for a job?" He seemed smart enough. And while he was undoubtedly a talented musician, was he really planning on a playing in a cover band for the rest of his life?

Stop judging, she reminded herself.

"I've got other stuff," he said. "But it requires me to be in the city too."

She waited. "Okay. Do I have to pry it out of you? Or is it like, if you told me you'd have to kill me?"

Everett scratched his neck. "Nah, nothing like that. I do some writing. Just some science stuff," he said.

"Science stuff? Well, that explains why you sound like a textbook." Now she was really intrigued. Everett wasn't making it easy for her to pull back the layers, though.

"It's pretty boring. Nothing glamorous and exciting like working at a law firm."

"Ha!" Jeannie said. "I'm afraid my job is more dry and boring than you might think." She gazed up at the faint green glow in the sky, more relaxed and open than she'd felt in a long time. "Sometimes I think I got into the wrong career. But I put so much time and effort into it that it feels too late to turn back. Seven years of university. And all the hours of overtime trying to prove myself. It's been a slog. Plus, I don't even know what else I'd do."

"Well. What makes you the happiest?" Everett poked the fire with a long stick, sending a spray of sparks into the dark night air.

"Nothing I could make an income from."

"Okay, put the money aside for a second. What's something you could do every day of your life, something that would make you leap out of bed in the morning?"

She thought back to the other morning spent in the kitchen, how she'd lost all track of time while mixing and rolling and tipping beautiful creations onto cooling racks. "I'd bake," she said. "Well, cook and bake. I love being in the kitchen."

"You can make money doing that."

"Sure. But—" She paused.

"Not enough money. You like your creature comforts."

"Is there anything wrong with that?" He might think she was shallow, but she liked the feeling of bringing in a good paycheck for all the hard work she did. And it meant she could buy herself a nice pair of shoes or go for a great dinner with Margot whenever she wanted, which was important to her.

"Not at all."

"Well, what about you? What would you do if money weren't an object?"

"I'd walk in the woods."

Jeannie burst out laughing. "So what, you'd pick up a hiking stick and just walk around alone in the trees aimlessly?"

"I don't know why you're laughing. We're talking about the things that make us happy. That's my happy place. The most wonderful place in the world. And I wouldn't have to be alone." He glanced over at her, a playful expression in his eyes. "You could come with me."

The woods behind the Butterfly Lake Lodge were just about the most beautiful woods around as far as Jeannie was concerned, thick with lodgepole pine and whitebark, Douglas fir and trembling aspen. She was hit with a pang of regret knowing that soon those woods would belong to someone else. Jeannie took a deep breath in, and a rush of impulse overtook her. So she was more of an indoor person. She still knew the forest like the back of her hand, and she knew Everett would love it. She wanted to bring him there.

"Let's go. Right now," she said, feeling brave and reckless and turned on. "I'll get some headlamps. I want to show you something." Her parents had returned to their home, Sue and Duke were asleep, and the boarders had gone back to their rooms, so no one would miss them.

Everett raised an eyebrow. "You've just outed yourself as a princess. It's the middle of the night. And it's winter." He looked her up and down. "What's under your jacket? If it's that sparkly red dress, I don't think it's going to be warm enough. And the snow's pretty deep. Plus," he said, "we only just met two days ago. Do you trust a stranger, all alone in the woods?"

She did, actually. Maybe it was unfounded, but she trusted him implicitly. And she wasn't just a corporate city girl. "Come with me. We just have to be quiet."

Chapter Eleven

IN THE MUDROOM off the side of the entrance to the lodge, Everett watched Jeannie pluck gear from piles of items organised in baskets. "My grandparents have collected a lot of stuff over the years," she whispered. "A lot of their boarders can't be bothered to pay the extra fees to ship all their gear back home, so they leave most of it here."

They got fitted up with headlamps, poles, snowshoes, and neck warmers, although after a few minutes of moving through snow that deep, they'd warm up anyway. Everett would have been okay to stay back and continue talking by the fire. Or stay in this dim room, all alone, and not talk. But he'd follow her lead.

Jeannie might label herself a "creature comforts kind of gal," but he liked this spontaneous, adventurous side of her. And she clearly knew more than she let on about the outdoors and being outside. She was just getting better by the second. *But she still thinks you're of a different class*, he reminded himself. And if she ever met his family, she'd probably turn around and run. They were nothing like hers, a family right out of the movies. He couldn't let himself get too stuck on her.

"And here," Jeannie said, passing him a small canister and tucking one in her own pocket. "Bears are hibernating, but after last night's excitement we're better to be safe than sorry."

"Agreed," said Everett. "All right. Let's go."

Fifteen minutes later, they were snowshoeing at a leisurely pace through the woods behind the lodge, not talking much except when Jeannie pointed out some landmarks—like the meadow in the middle of the forest that gave Butterfly Lake its name, where knapweed thistles, heather, and willowherbs grew thick and attracted thousands of butterflies in the warmer weather—and when Everett managed to spot a snowy owl high in the tree canopy above.

The air tasted of the recent snowfall, which coated the tree branches like fondant icing. How had he let himself stay away from this world for so long? He knew exactly why. For every perfect revelation from Mother Nature there was a pain in his heart for his father, who'd been so attuned to the natural world and all the things that brought Everett joy and exhilaration. In some ways, being outdoors made him feel closer to his father, but in another way, it made Everett miss him so much he felt sick.

He cleared his throat. He was out here with a gorgeous woman. He'd focus on her and the beauty of the moment. "Look," said Everett, pointing out some tracks in the snow lit up by his headlamp. They were pointy and heart shaped, separated down the middle like a broken heart.

"Deer," Jeannie said easily.

"You got it," he said. A whip-smart stunner who loved her family, wore high heels, drank beer from the bottle, and could ID tracks in the woods. Was he dreaming?

Now that they were farther out from the town and the faint light pollution from the small community, the stars shone even brighter in the sky above. "Let's rest for a second," Jeannie said. She stuck her poles into the snow by a tree and lay back on the snow in a small clearing. "I used to do this as a kid," she said. "Come here."

Everett put his poles next to hers and lay back in the snow beside Jeannie, closer than she might have expected him to. Should he move over? He shifted in the snow, and she didn't flinch. "Turn off your headlamp," Jeannie said, and Everett followed her instruction. Through the tall spindly evergreens and the leafless trees, the stars sparkled more brightly than as long as he could remember, and for several minutes they were quiet, the only sound coming from the gentle wind through the trees and their breathing.

"Is this what wanted to show me?" Everett asked after a few minutes. "It's amazing."

"Yes, but there's something else. It's back toward town. Come on," she said.

Jeannie led the way through the woods until they emerged behind the post office on the town's Main Street. The plows hadn't made it there yet, so the only way to tell where the road was located was from the gap in between the buildings. They passed the dark shops, the library, and the community centre until they reached a large pavilion. "Here," she said.

"What is it?"

Everett shone his headlamp into the covered area, and as they got closer, he made out a whole collection of ice sculptures, everything from a giant Christmas tree, to a bear holding a gift, to an intricately carved version of Santa's sleigh. The pavilion overhead had kept the snow off, though there were light drifts on the ground below. "This is incredible," he said. He turned to Jeannie. "I think this town is officially the most Christmas-y place on the planet."

"Agreed," Jeannie said. They walked through the sculptures, their headlamps making the ice sparkle and glisten. "What time do you think it is?" she asked. It was definitely way after midnight.

"I'd guess around one-thirty?" he said. If anyone had asked him a few days ago how he'd have pictured his Christmas, nothing about this night would have entered into his response. "We'd better be getting back."

JEANNIE WAS HAVING a great time and would have stayed out later with Everett, but he was right. It was really late, and the temperature was continuing to drop. She gestured the direction they needed to go.

"You know, you surprised me," Everett said. "I didn't peg you as someone with much of a sense of adventure."

"There you go again, making assumptions," she said. "But you're not entirely wrong. My work requires me to fit into a pretty narrow box. So, I don't often get to go snowshoeing in the middle of the night with guitar players."

"So, I'm the lucky anomaly, then."

Something about Everett made her want to shed her sense of propriety. Of what was expected of her. To do whatever the heck she felt like doing in the moment. And what she wanted to do in that very moment was to kiss him. She looked over to find his face lit up by the bright moon. "So, if it's after midnight, that means it's not Christmas anymore," she said.

Everett stopped and faced her, and she had no doubt in her mind what he wanted. She wanted it too.

"It's Christmas while we're still awake. Merry Christmas, Jeannie," Everett said quietly, and in a moment his lips were on hers, warm and soft. She could taste the sweet cider on his lips, and while there was a light stubble on his lip and chin, she couldn't get close enough to him.

She dropped her poles in the snow and allowed him to pull her in flush against his tall, lean frame. Kissing Everett McCarthy was a dream. She suddenly felt like a teen fan, kissing her music idol in some kind of far-fetched fantasy where he finally discovered she was the one in the audience who held the key to his heart.

Before midnight, after midnight, she didn't care. All that mattered was the way his lips moved with hers, the soft rumble of pleasure that seemed to come from deep in his chest, and the desire in his eyes when they pulled back for just a moment before melting back into an even deeper, hungrier kiss.

He kissed her like he wanted to make sure she'd never kiss anyone but him ever again. It must have been fifteen below, but every part of Jeannie burned with hot desire for Everett. Even through her thick layers of clothing, she felt his hands on her as though he were touching her bare skin. She let out an involuntary gasp as fingers, which had shed his glove at some point, moved down the back of her neck, then the side, bringing her closer still, until he moved his hand away and his lips were on that same spot, the trail of warmth setting her even further on fire.

Pieces of snow from her toque entered through her neckline and started to drip cold water down her back. It wasn't entirely unwelcome. She was burning up.

He pulled back, dipping his chin and fixing her in his gaze. He wanted her just as badly; there was no question. "We really should go back," he said, and her bubble deflated immediately. Did he think she was a bad kisser? Had she misread him completely?

She tried to catch her breath. "Uh, okay," she managed.

"It's not… It's just that—" He paused. He took her

hand, and reluctantly she pulled away a bit farther, trying to get to a place where she could think straight again. "I don't want your family to think I'm some kind of loser musician cliché," he said.

"I don't know why you'd—"

He grasped her other hand and looked her straight in the eye. "I really like your family. They're great people. And if they see you coming back with me like this, in the middle of the night," he said, "they may not like me quite as much." Jeannie knew he was right, even though she didn't want it to be true. She was twenty-eight and free to do what she wanted whenever she wanted, but no one wanted to wonder about their daughter or granddaughter's sex life. He passed her the hiking poles, and she allowed him to put the headlamp back on her head. "So, I need to get you back home before someone sees that the only thing on my bed right now is my brand-new hockey jersey."

Jeannie couldn't help but smile. "All right," she said. She knew everyone would be fast asleep. But it was sweet that Everett cared what her family thought of him.

"Let's go back," he said. "But let's keep our lamps off. You're right. It's magic out here."

With his poles tucked under one arm, he took her gloved hand in his. Under the light of the moon, they trekked back through the trees together and quietly let themselves back into the mudroom.

THE LODGE WAS quiet and still as they shed their outdoor gear.

"Cute pj's," Everett whispered, eyeing her fleece set with a grin on his face.

"Thanks, they're new," she said quietly, slightly embarrassed he was seeing her in her reindeer-print ensemble.

"Let me guess. The whole family has a matching set."

"You're not wrong."

Sue had left Everett's lamp on in his ground-floor room.

"I guess this is me," he said quietly in her ear.

"I feel like I'm dropping you off from a date," she whispered.

"Nice try. That wasn't the date," he said. He slipped his hand around her waist and drew her close. "But I'll take a goodnight kiss," he said quietly in her ear, his deep voice reverberating through every inch of her body.

"Goodnight, Everett," she breathed. His face turned, and his lips were on hers again, warm and wanting. She sighed with pleasure, shivering as his hand slid underneath the fabric of her pyjamas, holding the lower part of her back and trailing slowly upward.

A creek in the wooden floorboards above made them jump back. Jeannie stifled a giggle, then put a finger in front of her mouth, imploring him to stay quiet. "Goodnight," she whispered again and let go of Everett's hand. Who was awake?

She smoothed her pyjama top and took a steadying breath before ascending the stairs, hoping there were no creaks in the wood. Her entire body was buzzing with desire, and it was all she could do to keep moving forward instead of retracing her steps back into Everett's arms.

"What are you still doing up?"

Jeannie stopped in her tracks to find Sue in her white nightgown, white hair loose around her shoulders instead of in her usual bun. "I was just… I was worried I left the stove on," she fibbed. "I made tea after the movie."

Sue studied Jeannie's face. "You get some sleep," Sue said.

Jeannie nodded and started toward her room.

"And Jeannie," Sue said. "I said it before, and I'll say it again." She paused for a moment, then gave Jeannie a knowing smile. "He's a real sweetie. To think I'd been calling the wrong number for CAA all day! No wonder no one was calling me back." She winked.

Jeannie's jaw dropped. She stood looking at her grandma incredulously as Sue slipped back into her bedroom and shut the door.

Jeannie scoffed, unable to keep the wide grin from spreading over her face, then went in her room and shut the door, flopping onto her bed and burying her face in her pillow to muffle her laughter.

Chapter Twelve

BOXING DAY BREAKFAST was quiet and lazy, with people entering the kitchen at different times, some up bright and early to get the croissants at their warmest, and others indulging in a sleep-in after the busy festivities of the previous day.

When Jeannie descended to the kitchen, she found Everett deep in conversation with her grandfather debating the best track from The Beatles' *White Album*. Jim was already out on the rink with Lyndsay, and Gloria was doing a cross-stitch by the fire.

"There she is," Sue said. "Glad you slept in a little. CAA has already come and gone. I don't know what the problem was, but they seemed to have fixed it. The car's ready for Everett to drive back to the city." She winked at Jeannie. All Jeannie could do was shake her head at the extent of her grandmother's matchmaking mischief.

When the phone rang and Duke excused himself to take the call in the office, Jeannie took the opportunity to slide into his seat across from Everett, who was sipping his coffee, hair a little messed up from sleep in a very appealing way.

"Good morning," she said. From the other side of the table, the corners of Everett's mouth turned up in a delicious grin, and the idea of kissing him good morning was far more appealing than any of the golden pastries in the basket in front of her.

"Morning, Jeannie."

She barely noticed Sue beeline out of the kitchen.

Jeannie liked Everett. She liked how easily he fit in with her family and how he always had something interesting to say. She liked that he noticed things about her and seemed to be able to tell what she was thinking. She liked—well—pretty much everything about him.

So, he was a musician. Maybe that wasn't such a terrible thing. Maybe it would be fun to go out with him in the city. Maybe—

"Phone's for you," Duke called into the kitchen, interrupting her reverie.

"For me?" asked Jeannie. Who would be calling her at the lodge? The only person who knew where she was would be Laura. Hopefully nothing was wrong with Jazzy the cat.

"I'll be right back," she said, and Everett lifted his coffee in an adorable salute.

The rotary phone receiver sat off the hook on the office desk. "Hello?" she said.

"Hey, Jeannie," a familiar male voice sounded through the receiver.

It couldn't be.

"Ben?" asked Jeannie. She stretched the phone cord to shut the office door. "How did you—"

"I remembered the name of the place you were staying for Christmas and called the operator. Merry Christmas, by the way. Was Santa good to you?"

Ben Kane was calling? *Why?*

She cleared her throat. "He was," she said. "How about you?"

Ben chuckled. "Always a stand-up guy. Listen, when are you heading back to the city?"

Jeannie couldn't believe her ears. Was Ben finally asking her out? But what about the floozy at the bar? Or had she had too much to drink and misread the situation? "This morning, actually," she said, her pulse quickening. She'd be home by the early afternoon.

"I'm not sure if you have any plans on New Year's Eve," his deep, confident voice said through the receiver. "But there's this thing at my parents' club. It's a fancy event, and it's a lot of fun. I wanted to see if you'd be my date."

"What about that bartender?" Jeannie heard herself say. She couldn't help it.

"Who?"

"From the Tartan?" Jeannie asked. She winced. What a stupid thing to bring up.

"Oh, her? She's nothing," Ben said. "Not really right for that type of event anyway."

It bothered her that the bartender was so easily dismissed, but the fact that Ben saw her as something more gave her a rush of confidence. He considered her to be someone who fit into his world.

"I'd love to be your date," she said, already making plans in her mind for what shoes she already had, how she would do her hair, and where she'd go shopping for a dress. It would have to be at a less expensive store, given that she'd already spent her bonus on Everett's band.

Everett.

A punch of guilt hit her in the gut. But they'd just met. Sure, they'd shared a great kiss. And there was no denying that there was a connection between them. But Ben was just…right. In all the ways that mattered.

"I'll pick you up in a taxi at eight p.m. What's your address?"

Jeannie told Ben how to find her apartment building and gave him her home phone number. After hanging up, she sat back at the office desk, weighed down by a mixture of excitement and apprehension.

The Grey Spruce Golf and Country Club. Fabulous food and drinks, the who's who of the social scene, and maybe, if things went well, someone to buy her roses on Valentine's Day.

This Christmas may not have gone entirely according to plan. But New Year's Eve was shaping up to be a different story.

AFTER THEY'D BOTH packed their things in their cars and said goodbye to the boarders and the Carmichaels, Jeannie and Everett stood between their two vehicles.

"Thanks again for everything," she said. "You saved the party. You made it a close game. Everyone loved you."

"Spend New Year's Eve with me," Everett said, reaching over and taking her hand, his eyes alight with care and intention. "We're playing the pub again. It would be fun to have you there." Jeannie experienced a sudden irresistible urge to kiss him again. To invite herself over to his apartment to see his record collection. To walk in the park, and talk, and go to dinner, and then not talk. But she couldn't lead him on any further. It was cruel.

"I—I have plans on New Year's," she said. The second the words came out of her mouth, she felt like a fraud. What was she doing, turning down an invitation from this amazing man?

"Not the guy from the party," Everett said. She could tell he was doing his best to mask his disappointment.

"No," she said. Hot nerves and guilt uncoiled in her stomach. "Someone from work."

"Ah, the pretty boy," Everett said. His face crumpled slightly, then lifted into a fake grin. He opened the door to Erik's car, and Jeannie was desperate to get him to stay, to explain herself. "Well, Happy New Year's, Jeannie," he said.

He slid into the driver's seat. Her heart pounded. He was about to drive away. She had to explain herself. But then the car door opened again, and Everett ducked his head out.

"That thing I wanted to show you," he said. "The Celestial Cascade. It's supposed to be so bright this New Year's we'll see it even from the city. In case you want to make another wish."

Before she could say a word, Everett closed the car door, and Jeannie watched as he turned on the now-operational ignition, did a three-point turn, then disappeared down the lane to the main road.

Chapter Thirteen

JEANNIE COULDN'T CALM the butterflies in her stomach as she got ready for the party at the Grey Spruce on New Year's Eve. All day she'd been nervous, and she'd tried everything. Deep breathing. Reading a P.D. James mystery. She could barely manage two bites of the ham and Swiss sandwich she'd bought from the deli across the street in case the nerves were really just hunger pangs.

Ben was scheduled to pick her up in less than twenty minutes, but she'd been ready to go for over an hour. Dressed and made up, at least. The extra time with nothing to do only gave her the opportunity to worry about committing some kind of social faux pas that she didn't even know was gauche.

For the tenth time in the past half hour, she got up and inspected herself in the mirror.

Her dress, a colour-block black-and-white halter gown she'd found on a good sale from The Spot at Stephen Avenue Mall two days earlier showed off her figure nicely while also being appropriate for meeting Ben's parents, who she was sure would be in attendance. Her hair was swept away from her face and secured with a delicate silver comb. With a light make-up application and her mom's drop pearl earrings dangling above her shoulders, she looked her best and hoped Ben would think the same.

And for the hundredth time that hour, she did her best to push the image of Everett McCarthy, face lit up by the moonlight and eyes sparkling in the moment before he kissed her, right out of her mind.

When the doorbell finally rang, she pulled on her heavy wool coat, slid into her black pumps, praying it wouldn't snow while they were at the party, and opened the front door to find Ben in a black suit and overcoat, holding a bouquet of pink roses and grinning his thousand-watt grin, a cab idling on the street. *Good start*, she thought.

He held out the flowers. "You look great, Jeannie," he said. "All set?"

"I'll just put those inside," she said, accepting the flowers. "Feel free to come in."

"I'll wait here," said Ben.

She dropped the roses in a vase, then joined Ben back on the stoop. He extended an elbow for her and then led her to the taxi, where he opened the door in a very gentlemanly manner.

On the drive over to the Grey Spruce, Ben asked about her Christmas with her family. She told him about some of their traditions and a little bit about the party, but she found herself glossing over the details. Would he find it strange that her grandparents ran a boarding house? Would he say something condescending about the hockey tournament? Most of all, she didn't want him to know she'd spent most of her Christmas getting to know the guitar player from the pub band.

She turned her attention back to Ben, who was telling her about the ski conditions at Fernie and some kind of trick he'd pulled off on the moguls.

It wasn't long before they were checking in at the gate of the Grey Spruce, the security attendant waving them through as soon as he saw Ben in the back seat of the cab. "Nice to see you, Mr. Kane," said the man. "Your parents have already arrived."

So, he was a recognised guest.

"Thanks, George," said Ben.

"It's, uh, actually Jerry," the man said, then appeared embarrassed to have corrected Ben. He gave a wave and lifted the gate, and the cab continued to drive.

Ben was unfazed. "Jerry, George, what's the difference, right?" he said to Jeannie once they'd passed the gate. "Just let us through!" He laughed.

Jeannie forced a smile. *A little snooty*, she thought before her focus immediately shifted to the opulence and beauty of the club's grounds appearing out the taxi's windows.

The driver guided them along the winding path leading to the stately club, which was lit up with what seemed to be thousands of sparkling white lights and a giant halogen *1979* sign above the main entrance.

"This is stunning," Jeannie exclaimed. She stepped out of the cab, marvelling at the golden glow that surrounded the estate like a halo.

"Yeah, it's all right," Ben said, chuckling.

Jeannie's cheeks burned, and she chastised herself for being so effusive. She vowed to be more conscious about fitting in, starting with keeping her thoughts to herself.

But the gowns! The music! The buffet! The club was every bit as impressive as Jeannie could have imagined. The room was abuzz with the feeling of power and prestige and luxury. Jeannie tried not to stare when the prime minister walked in with his wife on his arm, but she noticed the other guests gawking, which made her feel like less of an outsider.

She met Ben's parents—Arthur, a CFO of an oil company, and Madeline, who complimented Jeannie's gown. Jeannie noticed Ben's mom shooting him a look of approval, which upped her confidence even further.

They sipped champagne, nibbled on smoked salmon and caviar, and watched the big band. When the band started to play "Fly Me to the Moon," Jeannie took Ben's elbow. "I love this song," she said. "Want to dance?" It wasn't Donna Summers, but it was classic and upbeat and perfect for the event and surroundings.

Ben grimaced. "I don't dance," he said. "Look, it's all the old people out there anyway."

Jeannie's cheeks burned anew. Now that he pointed it

out, all of the younger people at the party were at the bar or sitting at tables chatting over drinks. "Okay," she said.

Ben lifted his chin, searching the crowd. "There's my friend Hank from high school. Let's go say hi."

Jeannie followed Ben and stood behind him while he shook Hank's hand, then motioned for a member of the waitstaff to bring them some drinks.

"Who's this?" Hank asked, noticing Jeannie standing behind Ben. He introduced himself politely, but after that it was like she was invisible. Jeannie waited for Ben to include her in the conversation, but after several minutes of standing awkwardly by his side, nodding and smiling, she got bored and decided to walk around a bit. When she wandered away from Ben, he didn't even seem to register her departure.

Her heels were starting to pinch her feet a bit, so she found a deep armchair in a dim corner and sat in it and spent the next few minutes people watching until she saw Ben weaving his way through the crowd with a couple of other guys. "Ben," she called, and gave him a quick wave.

At first he looked at her as though he didn't even recognise her. "Oh, hey," he said. He'd unbuttoned the top button of his dress shirt, and with his cheeks a bit flushed, there was something boyishly handsome about him. She sat up, waiting for him to ask her to join him, or maybe invite her to the other room to look at the silent auction items. It would be fun to see what bids had been placed so far and guess what the items would end up selling for. "You're okay here, right? We're just going to go to the cigar lounge for a few minutes. Paul here has some Montecristos from Cuba."

Jeannie swallowed. How long would *that* take? She didn't know anyone else at the party, and Ben wasn't making a real effort to introduce her to anyone she might have something in common with. "Sure," she said weakly, then sat back in her chair as Ben followed his friends out of the room. *Boyish indeed.*

What was she supposed to do, sit alone all night, watching other people have fun? Why had he even invited her in the first place? Just to check the box of having a date? A lump formed in her throat, and her mind flashed to the dance floor at the Butterfly Lake Lodge on Christmas Eve, Everett's arms holding her firmly against him, his gaze fixed on her. The firepit on Christmas night when he'd hung on every word she'd had to say as though he thought she was the most special person in the entire world. The look in his eyes when she'd told him she had other plans on New Year's Eve.

She had to swallow to keep her eyes from brimming with tears. What had she done?

Jeannie spotted a circular balcony overlooking the event space and decided to climb the wide carpeted staircase that led to the second floor of the country club.

She stood alone for a few minutes, heart heavy, observing the party below her. Everything was exactly as she had imagined. The club was impressive. The food was exquisite. The guests all looked as though they'd walked out of a fashion magazine, or at least as though they could afford anything in its pages.

All in all, the evening was perfect.

Perfect on paper.

But suddenly, Jeannie was hit with the recognition that while everything was very nice, it was also very stuffy and very, very boring. And Ben Kane was a god-awful date.

She glanced at the grandfather clock behind her, then waved down a member of the waitstaff passing by with a tray of empty glasses and cocktail plates. "There's a man in the smoking lounge," Jeannie said to him. "Tall, blond hair, black suit. Will you tell him Jeannie wasn't feeling well and is in a taxi on her way home?" *Assuming he even cares*, she thought. Or that the waiter would be able to pick him out of the sea of other guys who looked exactly like him.

"Certainly, miss," he said. "Can I help arrange a car for you?"

"I'll be all right," Jeannie said, digging in her purse and pulling out a couple of dollars for the waiter. "Happy New Year." She found another staircase that led her to the foyer without her having to walk through the party.

Five minutes later, Jeannie had collected her jacket from the coat check and had slid into a cab, a rare feat on New Year's Eve, but the long line of taxis parked in front of the club told her there was a group of drivers counting on big tips from the wealthy club members.

She stared out the window as the cab navigated away

from the club toward downtown, then up at the sky, and had to blink when she realized what she was seeing overhead.

Perfectly imperfect. She heard Everett's voice in her head.

She reached into her purse and applied a fresh coat of Cupid's Cranberry lipstick.

It had worked once before.

THE TRUMPET AND Tartan was packed. If the bylaw officer decided this was the night to make a visit, the pub's operating license would most definitely be revoked, but when Everett caught a glimpse of the owner across the room, a beer in each hand and a wide grin on his face, it was clear that the man was rolling the life dice that there wouldn't be a surprise New Year's Eve inspection. At least this close to midnight, which, Everett noticed when he checked his watch, was only twenty minutes away.

It had been a good show, with a lively crowd, but unlike other performances when the cortisol energised him, Everett couldn't wait to get home to bed.

He took a moment to duck out to the alleyway to catch a breath of fresh air to wake up before the final set of the night.

The heavy metal door clanked shut behind him, and he was alone in the space between the pub and the men's clothing store next door. Everett breathed in deeply, the air filled with the scent of cooking hot dogs from the stand across the street and salt staining the sidewalk. He looked up. Sure as he'd predicted, early signs of the Celestial Cascade had started to streak the sky overhead. It would be blazing in a few hours, but he'd be face down and fast asleep in his bed by then.

Ever since he'd bid Jeannie farewell in the lodge's parking lot on Boxing Day, he'd barely slept. Many times he'd picked up the phone to call her and realised the only number he had for her was for her law firm. He'd found the Butterfly Lake Lodge in the phone book to see if Sue or Duke would give him Jeannie's number, but the minute he got to the last digit of the number, he paused and remembered that she had his number, and if she had any interest in speaking with him, she'd call.

Jeannie. He pictured her hand in hand with the guy from her law firm, all six foot three of his preppy attention on her, and it felt all wrong. There was no use denying it, even though she'd moved on, that she mattered to him.

And so, in the same way that he did every holiday season, knowing the occasion wasn't for him but wanting others to enjoy, Everett looked up at the stars above and put a call out to the universe to wish that wherever she was, Jeannie was having a great New Year's. Then he ducked back into the warm, noisy pub.

THE PUB MANAGER gave them the signal that they were ten minutes away from the countdown. Jeannie would soon be kissing someone else.

The thought of Jeannie's lips sent a pulse of longing through Everett, and when he missed the cue for the next song, he turned to find Greg with a puzzled, frustrated expression on his face.

"Sorry," Everett mouthed, and resolved to focus on the rest of the set.

But the universe had other plans.

Because someone waving at the back of the room caught his eye. He had to squint through the bright lights, but after a few seconds there was no mistaking the beautiful woman grinning from ear to ear, more dressed up than anyone else in the pub. She could have been wearing a burlap sack and she'd still have been the most gorgeous person there, and now she was wading through the crowd toward him.

A rush of energy and desire struck him like a bolt of lightning, and after a quick sidebar conversation between songs, he launched into Cheap Trick's "I Want You to Want Me"—he might as well just be honest at this point—and watched as Jeannie laughed, then waved again, her gaze not once breaking from his.

And then in a swirl of lights and cheers and chanting, they were counting down from ten, and Everett was pulling Jeannie up on stage with the help of a couple of other concertgoers, careful not to rip her dress or have her stumble in her heels, and then she was in his arms, the whole pub chanting the countdown to the stroke of midnight. Jeannie's lips met his in a kiss that left Everett with no doubt that he would never kiss another woman again. And that the wish he'd made, even though it had made him feel like a crazy fool, was coming true.

"Happy New Year, Jeannie Carmichael," he said, her cheek warm against his. He held her close, his hand on her lower back, the silky fabric of her dress almost as touchable as the soft hair at the nape of her neck, which he trailed through with his other hand.

"Happy New Year, Everett," she whispered in his ear. "I've been thinking about that date."

"Uh huh," he said, waiting for her to say it.

"January 1st seems like a pretty good day for it."

"I couldn't think of anything better," he said, and they both jumped as a partygoer let a confetti tube explode right over the heads of everyone around them, a rain of gold glitter catching the light and falling onto their shoulders.

Jeannie had come to him. And he would do whatever he could to never let her go.

Epilogue

"FAMILY AND FRIENDS of the bride and groom," the minister's booming voice proclaimed to the guests assembled in the great room, "it is now my distinct pleasure to introduce to you for the first time, Mr. and Mrs. Everett and Jeannie McCarthy!"

The guests watched and cheered as Jeannie dipped back in Everett's arms. He took a moment to look deeply into her eyes before kissing her reverently. The room filled with the sound of both applause and Everett's band, accompanied by the jazz trio, from the stage at the back of the great room. When Jeannie's and Everett's lips parted and they pulled away, opening their eyes, they were both grinning like fools.

Jeannie gazed out at the sea of faces, taking in the sight of family, her friends, colleagues from the law firm, and members of the Keystone Ridge community. In the front row, next to Jeannie's parents and grandparents, were Everett's mother, bursting with pride in a red satin dress, and his sister, Jessie, who Everett was amazed and overjoyed had been able to drive up with Everett's mom for the occasion.

At the back of the room, three Aussies, who were now

living in a rented house close to Banff but were thrilled to have something to do on Christmas Eve, stood with trays of champagne ready to pass out to the guests.

As much as Jeannie loved them, she hoped they didn't have any plans to break into song this year.

She turned to her groom. Everett was more handsome than ever, wearing a navy suit with a green tie that looked formal and classic from afar but upon closer inspection had little leaves embroidered into it. His hair was combed back from his face, highlighting his cheekbones, and his brown eyes held her in the most loving of gazes.

They'd gotten engaged on a hike of the Grotto Mountain Trail over Thanksgiving weekend. Everett had packed a bottle of champagne for the hike, suggesting they could celebrate his new book contract which, Jeannie knew, her grandparents would proudly display beside the copies of his books they were delighted to find they already owned even before meeting him, hence Duke's unexplained name recognition of Everett. Instead, Everett had dropped to a knee before a large rock wall with a gentle waterfall cascading down its face.

They'd immediately set out on a campaign to convince her grandparents to hold one final event at the Butterfly Lake Lodge: their Christmas Eve wedding. It hadn't been hard to convince Duke and Sue, who were taking their time with the sale, citing a down market with the possibility of an upswing in the coming summer.

While the notion of getting married at the lodge had never crossed Jeannie's mind before she'd met Everett (if anyone had asked her she would have had some vague notion of a historic estate or country club with hundreds of guests and black tie), the day was turning out to be even dreamier than she'd ever imagined. It was elegant but unpretentious, with their closest family and friends and people from the community where they felt most at home, where Jeannie's most treasured life memories had been made, and where Everett had recently found some of his.

Once the champagne flutes were distributed, there was a toast to the bride and groom, and then passed hors d'oeuvres and music. The evening itself wasn't terribly different from the Carmichaels' usual Christmas Eve parties, but there were a few elegant but cheeky upgrades: a giant ice sculpture of an elk sparkled in the middle of the room, while a canoe filled with snow hosted a sea of shucked oysters, and just when everyone thought Sue couldn't be outdone, she wheeled out a giant pretzel cart that Duke had constructed to look like it came right out of a Bavarian market, with dipping sauces ranging from honey mustard to spinach-and-artichoke to dill pickle. Between that and Everett surprising Jeannie with a dance to "I Feel Love" under a disco ball she hadn't even noticed he'd hung from the rafters, she couldn't have hoped for a better night.

Later that evening as the reception was winding down and Jeannie had long since kicked off her high heels, Duke and Sue called Everett and Jeannie into the office and asked them to sit down. "This won't take long," Duke said, closing the door. "I know you'll want to get out there and say goodbye to the rest of your guests. But we can't stay up any longer."

Jeannie's heart swelled. Her grandfather especially had aged quite a bit over the past year, and she was so grateful that Everett loved coming to the lodge so much that they'd visited almost every weekend and she'd been able to spend so much quality time with her grandparents.

"We wanted to give you your gift," Sue said, sliding a manila envelope across the table. "And before you open it, we want to make it clear that you can do with it whatever you'd like. But we insist that it's something that will make you happy. Not something you think you *should* do."

"What is it?" Jeannie asked.

"Just open it," Duke said, a twinkle in his eye.

With Everett and her grandparents looking on, Jeannie unsealed the envelope and pulled out a document. It took her a moment to realise what she was holding in her hand. "Grandpa, Grandma, you can't—" She sat, her mouth gaping.

"We can. And we have," Sue said, beaming. "Sweetheart, we've had so many great years here. But we're moving, and we really can't bear to think of the place in someone else's hands."

"But what about the trip to Tahiti? The Orient Express?

Paris at New Year's? The sale was going to fund your retirement."

"Pff!" said Duke, waving his hand in the air. "You think we really want to do anything other than read on the front porch and play Tuesday night bingo at the Legion? And God willing"—he looked pointedly at Everett—"hold a great-grandbaby one day?"

Jeannie, speechless, passed the document to Everett, who blinked a few times as he scanned it. "You're giving us the lodge?" he asked. Jeannie watched as his expression went from confused to awestruck. "I—wow—I can't even—"

"It's yours as soon as we find the right place," Duke said. "We're going to take our time finding a good spot, something small that's close to town so we don't have to drive a lot. We just wanted to know that you'd accept first. You will, right? You can do what you want with the place. Live here. Weekend here. Just—" He paused and looked over at one of the photos on the wall. It was a young Duke and Sue standing in front of the FOR SALE sign the day they'd purchased the lodge. "Just don't sell it right away," he said. "Something tells me you'll come to love the lodge even more once it's yours."

Tears brimmed in Jeannie's eyes, and she almost leapt across the desk to hug her grandparents. "Why would we ever sell this place?" she said, still struck with disbelief at the enormity of the gift. It had always felt like home. And now it was theirs.

Everett's expression was still one of pure shock. Jeannie knew how much he'd come to love the lodge, and they'd recently been talking about the idea of buying a small cottage in the area with the advance from the sale of his new nature guide series, or even building one of their own. But waterfront property was at a major premium, so in their minds the idea had been something in the woods that would at least allow them to walk to the water to swim. Now they'd be the stewards of a place that occupied what might be one of the most magical locations in the whole country. It defied belief.

"You promise you're going to keep living close to here though, right?" Jeannie asked. The idea of Keystone Ridge without her grandparents wasn't something she could ever imagine.

"The furthest we'd go is Canmore," Sue said. "So, we'll be close by. With a property manager to take care of the shovelling! Now, you get back out there," Sue said. "Your guests are waiting."

They hugged her grandparents again, and, hand-in-hand, went back to the wedding reception in the beautiful lodge they would now call home.

AFTER EVERYONE HAD gone to bed, Jeannie and Everett changed out of their wedding attire, bundled up, and went outside the way they had only one year earlier.

The snow was deep and thick, but with their snowshoes on they stayed close to the top layer, the stars bright in the clear sky overhead.

"I still can't believe your grandparents," Everett said. "Do you think that was their plan all along?"

"Not sure," Jeannie said. "Although I wouldn't be surprised." It still hadn't sunk in. The lodge would be *theirs*. "Do you think they have any expectations for how we use it?"

"They don't strike me as that kind of people. I think they just want you to be happy. And I guess they don't need the money."

They'd reached the edge of the lake where the path led through the forest into town. "Do you remember what we were talking about last year, right here?"

"What part?" Everett asked. "About making a quinzhee and having a hot sleepover?"

Jeannie laughed and swatted him. "No! You know what I'm talking about."

"Okay, okay. You mean what we'd do if money weren't a consideration?"

Jeannie nodded.

"You'd bake all day, and I'd walk in the woods?"

Jeannie grabbed his hand. "But what if we could actually do that? You know how I've been feeling about my job. And you can write anywhere."

"I suppose we could. But that's a lot of house for two

people."

"No, I mean—what if we turn it into a hotel or something? We could redo the bedrooms, add some bathrooms. I can serve breakfast and happy hour snacks. You could organise wilderness tours. Share your love of the area with guests. What do you think?"

For a moment, she was terrified that he'd say no. That it was a stupid idea. Because the truth was as soon as the words escaped her mouth, there was nothing in the world Jeannie wanted to do more. But there was something else she needed to spill. "We should at least talk about it. Is it midnight yet?" she asked Everett.

He checked his watch and nodded. "Merry Christmas, Wife," he said. He stopped in a snowy clearing and leaned over to kiss her.

Jeannie sighed contentedly. *Wife.* She loved being his wife. And there was another title she'd be taking on soon. "I've been waiting until it's officially Christmas to give you your gift," she said.

He looked down at her gloved hands, which were empty.

"We're having a baby," she whispered, choking up over the sight of absolute glee that washed over Everett's face in the faint light of the moon.

"What? I can't—" He shook his head. "I feel like I'm dreaming."

"It's early. But I took a test and..." She grinned. "I've got a doctor's appointment booked for the twenty-ninth."

She'd woken up a week earlier with a terrible sense of nausea, breasts tender, and the slightest bit of brain fog, and had felt under the weather ever since. She'd initially attributed it to the business of working and planning the wedding and being just plain exhausted, until she realised she was late and had gone down to the drugstore at lunch to buy a pregnancy test. Despite the shock, she'd laughed to herself when she realised that a year earlier to the day she'd left at lunch to buy a lipstick. "And I feel like it's a girl. I can sense it."

Everett picked her up and twirled her. "I didn't know it was possible to be this happy," he said, pulling her in close. "The Butterfly Lake Lodge. Will people come?"

"I guess we'll see," Jeannie said, laying her head on Everett's shoulder and picking the biggest and brightest star in the sky to make a wish.

But her dream, she realised, had already come true the moment Everett McCarthy had walked into her life.

If this wasn't perfect, she didn't know what was.

The End

If you enjoyed *Wish Upon A Christmas Star*,
you'll love the other books in the…

The McCarthy Sisters series

Book 1: *Wish Upon A Christmas Star*

Book 2: *The Wedding Twist*

Available now at your favorite online retailer!

About the Author

Elle Douglas writes small-town contemporary romance for lovers of warm, feel-good stories that are on the sweeter side. Her novels feature strong, relatable characters living in tight-knit communities, with a backdrop of stunning Canadian wilderness.

Elle is a lover of 90's alternative music, a wannabe chef specializing in comfort food and a sometimes reluctant but usually dedicated gym-goer who lives in Toronto with her wife and their cat Lucy (or Lucifer, depending on the day). Between writing romance novels and working as a high school guidance counsellor, Elle works exclusively in helping others find their happily-ever-afters.

She is a graduate of TMU's Radio and Television Arts program, OISE at the University of Toronto, and the University of Toronto Creative Writing program, and is a member of Toronto Romance Writers, Romance Writers of America and Georgia Romance Writers.

Thank you for reading

Wish Upon A Christmas Star

If you enjoyed this book, you can find more from all our great authors at TulePublishing.com, or from your favorite online retailer.

TULE
PUBLISHING

Printed in the USA
CPSIA information can be obtained
at www.ICGtesting.com
LVHW090719031124
795554LV00036B/820

9 781964 703824